the Island Bookshop

CORAL ISLAND
BOOK FIVE

LILLY MIRREN

black lab press

Read The Series In Order

One

THE ROOM WAS DARK. Only a vague reddish light showed the images coming to life on the paper held beneath the liquid's surface. Eveleigh Mair used a small pair of tongs to pick up the photography paper by the edge and lift it from the tray. She held it aloft a few moments as the excess fluid dripped back into the tray, her eyes squinting behind a pair of clear plastic goggles. Then she raised the image over her head and pegged it by one corner to a thin line of rope.

She must've been the only person on Coral Island who still used a film camera. She did it for artistic reasons — she loved the way photographs looked using film. She'd grown up taking photos with her mother's SLR and couldn't shake the habit, even though digital photos these days were so much easier to use and had amazing clarity. There was something special about the process of taking photos the old-fashioned way and developing them in her own darkroom behind the bookshop.

Her entire family thought she was crazy. Her mother had updated to using her phone for every captured memory years ago.

"Why go backwards?" she'd asked when Evie questioned her about it. Suddenly Evie had felt as though she was the oldest person in the world. It was a good question. Why? But she'd kept it up anyway because she enjoyed it. And these days, she didn't have many hobbies. Most of her time was spent running the business, a quaint old bookshop called *Eveleigh's Books*. She'd rented and fitted out the space with the nest egg she'd saved over many years. Another *crazy* initiative. Most people asked her why she didn't simply accept that people shopped online these days and read ebooks on their phones, but she liked holding on to the past. To her, tradition meant something, and she fully intended to maintain doing what she loved for as long as she could.

The photographs hanging above her head looked fearsome in the morbid lighting, but they were happy images — beachscapes, birdlife, the dock where ferries came to rest after bringing tourists to the shores of Coral Island on a daily basis, and then taking them back to the mainland again after sun-filled days in a tropical getaway.

Her clients were people like her—they loved to take film photographs, and since there were few studios with a dark-room in northern Queensland, they'd mail their film from near and far for her to develop on their behalf. It was a small but thriving niche business and she enjoyed the artistry it sometimes took, especially when developing old film canisters like the one Beatrice had found in her cottage's kitchen wall cavity. Maintaining the integrity of the images had been something of a challenge, and Evie had loved every minute of it.

Finished, she flicked the red glowing safe light on, and the bulb burst to life with a low hum. Then she set about packing everything away. With one last look of appreciation at the images, she picked up a basket full of items to take back to the kitchen with her — dirty coffee mugs and plates, a half-eaten bag of chips, an empty wine bottle for the recycling bin and the latest book she was reading.

As she pushed the darkroom's door shut with her behind, she heard a pounding sound coming outside the bookshop. With a frown, she considered ignoring it since her hands were full and she was exhausted after a long day of work, but in the end, she realised it might be a delivery of books. She was waiting on several boxes of the latest releases to put up in a display over the weekend, and she couldn't very well leave them sitting outside all night long.

The knocking had stopped. Hopefully, the delivery man had left the boxes on the porch. She hated when they pushed a card into the door and expected her to drive to the post office to pick them up after only missing them by a few seconds. Determined not to add to her to-do list the following day, she quickened her steps along the narrow corridor and through the small kitchen, then into the bookshop.

Just as she passed the register, her foot broke through the floorboards, and she went plummeting down with a squeal of fright. She landed on her rear end with one leg dangling through the floor. The basket she'd been carrying went flying across the room and landed with a disheartening smashing of china against the far wall.

Her eyes squeezed shut as pain shot up her leg. She squeaked in dismay and then gingerly felt along her limb as she slowly pulled the leg out of the hole. If it was broken, it would be a complete disaster. She had the busy season coming up — the winter months were when most of the tourists arrived on Coral Island. The delightfully warm weather and brilliant sunshine throughout the colder season was the perfect opportunity for holiday makers to fly north for the winter to escape the ice, driving rain and falling snow in the southern states.

Satisfied that she hadn't broken a bone, she studied the floorboard that had given way.

"What on earth?" It had rotted through. She'd known there was movement in some of the boards—she had noted it a few times and had seen some customers give the floor a questioning look every now and then. But it was an old building. Surely older buildings like this one always had a few rotten boards in them, but she'd had no idea that might mean she'd one day fall through and almost end up spread-eagled on the concrete foundations. Just thinking of the nasties that might be hidden below her timber floor sent a shiver up her spine. She could've landed feet first in a rat's nest, for all she knew. Although she did her best to make sure there were no rats beneath the bookshop, she supposed you could never be certain, and and apparently, you couldn't be certain that the ground wouldn't open up beneath you either.

There was another knock at the front door, this time a quiet tapping rather than the thunking of a fist that'd come before. Surely the delivery man had given up by now. She'd never known him to give more than a cursory thump before skedaddling down the stairs and back into his vehicle. He was always in a hurry, and she supposed that made sense given how much the postal service had cut back on staff in recent years. But it still frustrated her at times, and because of that she'd rushed to answer the door and fallen through her floorboards.

"Just a minute!" she shouted as she worked her leg out of the hole, grimacing at the pain in her knee.

She'd scraped her leg badly down the shin and the calf as well. She hobbled to open the door, then steadied herself by leaning against the wall briefly before pulling it open.

"Hi... sorry for the wait. I fell... Oh, you're not the postie."

A man with brown curly hair and dark brown eyes stood on the landing, both hands pushed deep into the pockets of his jeans.

"I'm David Ackerman, the new principal at the primary school across the street, and I thought I'd come check out the local bookshop. I'm an avid reader, and I'm passionate about getting kids into reading. Are you closed? I'm sorry—I've probably come at the exact wrong time." His face registered alarm. "Is that blood?"

"I was expecting the postman," she said.

His eyes narrowed. "Huh? The postman?" He bent to examine her leg. "You're definitely bleeding. What happened?"

She blinked. "I was trying to get to the door, and I fell through the floor. It's rotten and I've been meaning to get the boards fixed, but I hadn't gotten around to it. I should've made it more of a priority, but you know how these things go — you're juggling so many urgencies as a small business owner, it's hard to know which one to give your attention first."

"Lean on me, and let's get you inside," the man said, reaching for her arm and looping it around his waist. He was tall, and she felt tiny next to his looming frame. She did her best to hobble back into the bookshop, but within seconds, he'd swept her up into his arms and was carrying her across the shop and past the hole in the floor to the small kitchen, where he gently lowered her into a chair.

"Is this okay?"

She nodded silently. He'd picked her up as though she were a twig. She couldn't recall the last time she'd been carried. She was forty-six years old, and no one had picked her up since she was a child. It felt nice to be taken care of, but it caught her by surprise. She hoped he wasn't a serial killer or a robber— not that she ever kept much in the way of cash inside the shop. She tucked her red curls behind her ears.

"Thanks," she said.

He pulled a second chair towards her and raised her foot onto it, cradling it with tender hands. "You're welcome. Let's take a look and make sure nothing's broken. This is a pretty nasty cut."

"I don't think it's broken. Probably only bruised."

"Bruising we can deal with, although you may need a tetanus booster."

She clenched her teeth. "I hate needles."

"Oh, come on. It's not so bad. And we have no idea what kind of gremlins are in those floorboards. You might've been nicked by a rusty nail as well."

"You're probably right. Thank you for your help. I do appreciate it, although I'm sure you have much better things to do with your time than helping a middle-aged woman who is apparently now prone to falling."

"Middle-aged? I don't know about that. I'm forty-six, and I'm clinging to my youth by ignoring the progression entirely."

She laughed. "We're the same age, then."

"How about that?" His eyes twinkled. "I noticed the front door was hanging a little crooked on its hinges too, if you're getting things fixed."

She slapped a hand to her forehead. "This whole place is falling apart. It's in dire need of a facelift. I'm no good with tools, I'm afraid."

He scratched his chin. "I could fix the door, but you probably need more work done than that. It'd be a good idea to at least work on the floor. We can't have you falling through the boards regularly."

"I know I should do it, but it costs a lot of money, and besides, when? I work here all day every day."

He raised both hands as if in surrender. "I'm not going to tell you what to do, but please be more careful or I'll be forced to come check on you daily to make sure you're still alive."

She sighed. "I'm sorry. This isn't your problem to solve, it's mine. I'm being very rude."

She was horribly indecisive at times. It was why she never changed her life— instead, she just kept living exactly the same day over and over again because she didn't know how to make a change, and there was no one in her life to force her into it.

There was a sadness to her voice and it lingered in her throat. Was she living perpetually in Groundhog Day? Would she one day reach the end of her life and wonder what might've been, or what she could've done differently? She wasn't like Taya. Her friend amazed her with the way she'd seized hold of life as though it was one big adventure. Taya hadn't always been like that. She'd been frozen in grief and then in the busyness of motherhood for a long time. But now, she was blossoming into the woman Evie had always known she could be. But Evie felt stuck, as though she'd been left behind.

There were times when she was happy and confident as a single woman and entrepreneur, and at other times she wished she had a life partner — someone to talk to, to help make decisions, to sit and watch a movie or take a trip for the weekend.

"I don't mind at all," David said. "I'm great at input. Sometimes I give far too much—at least my sister says so."

Evie laughed.

"The postman left several boxes on the landing. I'll bring those inside for you."

She sighed. "Thank you — that would really help."

"Sit and rest."

Before long, she heard David bringing the boxes in from the front porch. She hobbled to the bench and set the kettle to boil. The least she could do was to have a cup of tea waiting for him when he finished.

One of the things she loved most about Coral Island were the relationships she had with the other residents. Having spent most of her life there, she knew almost everyone. They were salt-of-the-earth folks, people she could rely on in a time of need. She knew that, and the knowledge warmed her heart. And now a man she'd never met was helping out in her bookshop. He was clearly destined to live on the island—he'd fit right in. The people of Kellyville would love him. She wouldn't exchange her community for any amount of money. It was priceless.

As the kettle finished boiling, she sliced a pineapple upside-down cake and set pieces on two plates. Her phone rang, and she fished it out of her pocket. With the phone hugged to her ear by one shoulder, she answered without looking at the caller ID.

"Hello?"

"Hi, honey. It's Mum. How are you?"

She poured water into the teapot then shuffled back to her chair, lowering herself into it with a groan. "I've been better."

"What's wrong?" Mum asked immediately, concern making her tone abrupt.

"I fell through a rotten floorboard and grazed my leg pretty badly."

"That darned building—I told your father just the other day that it's going to fall down around your ears if you don't do something about it. Won't you let us help?"

Evie rubbed a hand over her face. "Thanks, Mum. I appreciate it—really, I do. But I can handle this."

"Will you, though? I can't stand the idea of you living in that place with it coming apart like that. I'll be worried every moment. I won't be able to sleep."

"Don't worry, Mum. I promise, I'm going to take care of it. The landlord isn't local and is utterly hopeless. So I'll figure something out myself. I'm going to have to hire a contractor. My friend Bea has a great one, and I'm sure I'll be able to get him to come in and make everything brand new again."

"Well...if you're sure. Otherwise, I'll be happy to come get you. You could stay with us a while, have a little holiday."

"Don't do that, Mum. I'm fine. Really, I am."

"Okay, good. In that case, I have a favour to ask."

Evie had walked directly into that one. She inhaled a breath and held it in her lungs, waiting.

"Your sister is home."

She exhaled. It wasn't a mystery where the conversation was headed once she knew Emily was staying with their parents. Now she understood the invitation to come and stay with them — they wanted her to keep Emily occupied. Without Evie to help, they wouldn't want her to be there for long. They'd push her on Evie, claiming the two of them needed to reconnect.

"She'd love to see you. She misses you so much. She's your twin, after all. Aren't twins supposed to have some kind of spiritual connection? And yet you act as though you don't have a sister. She feels rejected, Evie."

Evie covered her eyes with a palm and leaned forwards. "Oh, Mum, I'm sure she didn't say anything of the kind. She hasn't called me or come to see me in years. Why would she suddenly feel the need now?"

"You know how she is—she can't express her feelings well. But I know it's how she feels. She doesn't have to say the words outright."

Evie shook her head. Mum was making things up again. It'd be a cold day in hell before her sister would honestly admit to missing her.

"So, she wants to visit. Is that what you're saying? More likely, you want her to visit so she's out of your hair. She's no doubt driving you both crazy. Am I right?"

"Of course not," Mum fussed. "She's our daughter, and we love her unconditionally. But we'd appreciate it if you'd let her come stay with you for a while. And now that you're doing a renovation, you'll have time — maybe she could lend a hand. See, it's all working out perfectly. I'm glad I called."

Two

THE NEXT TUESDAY, once the last customer had left the bookshop, Evie went outside to sit on the landing. With a grunt, she lowered herself onto an old metal chair and raised her injured leg to let her foot rest on the railing. Another thing that needed to be fixed—it was remarkable the thing hadn't fallen to the ground the moment she pressed her foot to it. But it remained stubbornly in place, even if nothing held it together but a piece of rotten timber and a long, rusted nail.

The shop was blue with lilac trim. Beside her, a tall, rusted statue of a pelican had perched for as long as she could remember. The previous tenant had run a crystal shop with a beach theme, and from what she recalled, there'd been birds positioned throughout the store — glass, crystal, clay and steel sculptures — some big, some small, some suspended from the ceiling with string. The pelican was the only one she'd kept. Mostly because it was heavy and she couldn't lift it. But there was something regal about the old bird she liked as well.

She leaned back in her chair and opened the book on her lap. It was a story about a woman who travelled around Australia with a group of friends and the mishaps that occurred along the way. She flicked through the pages, stopping to read a paragraph here or there. It'd come highly recommended via the distributor she used to stock her shop, and she was considering assigning it as the *Book of the Month* at the next book club meeting.

Janice bounced through the front door, her long brown ponytail swinging.

"I'm off. See you tomorrow!"

"Thanks for all your help," Evie called after her.

She was grateful for Janice. The woman was in her early twenties and had limitless energy, plus a passion for books that meant the two of them could share in the excitement of opening a new box or the thrill of reorganising a shelf. The two of them had grown close in recent months and Evie wasn't sure how she'd manage without her now, even if she only worked part time. Janice had learned to run the bookshop when Evie was in her darkroom developing photos — a niche side gig Evie had taken on to help pay the rent.

She read for an hour before looking up again. By now, the sun had begun to set beyond the western horizon, brightening the dark ocean with a golden tint. Her thoughts wandered to her encounter with the new principal a week earlier. The school sat still and quiet across the street. The playground was empty, and there were only a few cars parked at the curb—no doubt the most conscientious teachers preparing for work the next day. But she hadn't seen David again since he knocked on her door and introduced himself.

The girls were coming over for dinner soon. Taya was back from an overseas trip for work, and Bea had returned from her honeymoon in Italy. Penny had been so busy lately with her animal refuge that Evie hadn't seen her in weeks. But that night, the four of them were finally getting together, and Evie couldn't wait.

She hobbled down the road to her quaint timber house.

She rarely locked the door, since crime was virtually nonexistent on the island. Of course, Mary Brown's killer, Buck Clements, was still loose after posting bail several weeks earlier. Perhaps she should start locking up again to be on the safe side.

The house was silent when she stepped inside. She'd left the windows open, and the scents of fresh-cut grass and salt were in the air. She flicked on a light switch and tied an apron around her neat waist. The last thing she always did before cooking was to fasten her red curls into a bun at the nape of her neck. She took her time, massaging the tired and cramped neck muscles that'd been tight ever since her fall. Then washed her hands.

One of her go-to meals was chicken enchiladas with Mexican rice and refried beans, along with a freshly cut side salad. It was simple and delicious, a recipe she'd honed over the years. She set about slicing onions and chicken, with a crooning montage of easy listening music playing in the background.

This season of life was good, even if she had been stuck in a rut for a while. She'd been something of a brooder in her twenties. That decade was characterised by bouts of passionate creativity interspersed with dark moods, broody self-consciousness, imposter syndrome whenever anything went better than she expected, and short-lived, tumultuous romantic relationships.

Her thirties had been better. She'd settled into a career as a photographer and had managed to pull a fairly consistent client list together that enabled her to not only pay the bills, but to save a small nest egg. She'd learned a few things about herself — what she was good at, what she should let go of— and had worked through the aspects of her childhood that had caused her to form some bad habits in her life with the help of a few counselling sessions.

The most notable aspect of that decade had been the development of a long-term, loving relationship with a man called Gareth. She'd thought they would be married and she had put all her effort into building a life with him. They'd dated for eight years, most of her thirties. All the while, she kept waiting for him to pop the question and wondering why he wouldn't. When she finally asked him about it, he said that he loved her, but he wasn't the marrying kind.

Almost a decade ago, he left her for another woman, and they were married within two months. It seemed he was the marrying kind after all, but Evie wasn't the kind he wanted to marry. His rejection had hurt her deeply, but she'd come to realise she didn't miss him so much as she missed the idea of what she thought they might've built together. She'd moved back to Coral Island, used her savings to set up the bookshop, and established a quiet, sheltered life for herself. But sometimes she wondered if perhaps she'd run away from life rather than towards it.

Footsteps on the path leading up to the front door brought her attention back to the present moment. She wiped her hands on the apron tied neatly around her waist.

Beatrice Rushton stepped through the door, a bottle of wine in one hand and her eyes sparkling. "It smells divine in here. What are you making?"

"Come on in!" Evie trilled, rushing to kiss her friend's cheeks.

She took the offered bottle and ushered Bea into the kitchen. "Take a seat if you like, or you can help me with this rice."

The rice maker had switched to "warm" and all Bea had to do was spoon it into a bowl, so she got to work doing that while they caught up on the day's news.

"How's your leg healing?" Bea asked as she set the bowl of

rice in the centre of the small, round dining table beneath a gable window.

"It's feeling a lot better. The bruising was the worst part, and it's not as painful today as it was a few days ago."

Just then, Taya and Penny arrived. They chattered loudly as they clattered across the hardwood floor in the living room. Taya brought a chocolate mousse for dessert, which she immediately set about rearranging Evie's refrigerator to house. And Penny brought chips and salsa.

Evie held up the chip packet. "We're eating Mexican food tonight, so this is perfect."

"I'm back on dairy," Bea said. "It didn't seem to help my allergies to go dairy-free, so I'm looking forward to eating all the cheese."

Evie laughed. "An excess of dairy, coming up!"

Finally, all four of the women sat around the table. Between them, steam rose from the large casserole dish of enchiladas, a bowl of seasoned rice and another of refried beans. The fresh salad was colourful, and when spooned onto plates, the entire meal look healthy and delicious. Evie had barely eaten a thing all day. She'd spent much of the morning in the darkroom. When she worked on developing photographs, she could focus for hours without realising how much time had passed. When she finally emerged to help Janice in the bookshop, they'd been overrun by a group of tourists, and she didn't get a chance to catch her breath until after closing. Now she was starving.

They ate between snippets of conversation and hoots of laughter. Evie loved how their friendship only deepened the more time that passed. They knew each other so well after so many years. These women were the only people on the planet she could be entirely herself around without insecurities or hesitation, and she knew they loved her regardless.

"I'm loving my work," Taya said as she dabbed a napkin to

her red lips. "It's so fulfilling and interesting. There's always something new and different for me to do. I never know what each day will bring, and the number of challenges I've already faced — well, if you'd told me ahead of time, I might not have done it. But the funny thing is, I've handled them all. And I feel good about that."

"I'm not one bit surprised," Evie said as she added salad to her plate. "I knew you'd be amazing. Besides, it runs in the family. Obviously, your dad is pretty adept at managing resorts or he wouldn't have such a hugely successful company."

Taya shrugged. "I suppose you're right. I never thought about it that way before — I don't think I've given him credit for all he's achieved. He's been a big success for most of my life, and I don't remember what it was like before that. I'm sure he worked long hours without much to show for it, but that must have happened when I was small. The only part of it I recall was that he wasn't around, and I held that against him for a long time."

"We all have our issues from childhood, even when our parents did a good job. I think that's part of living through your thirties and forties — you finally find peace about the way your parents raised you and realise they did the best they could," said Evie.

"You're right," Taya said. "I know my parents did—they were wonderful. Dad was gone much of the time, but he worked so hard to build a life for all of us. And he was there for me when I had to raise Camden on my own — he stepped up to be the father figure in her life. She's so well grounded, and I think a lot of that is because of my parents and their involvement."

"And because of you. You're a great mother. No doubt you learned that from them," Penny said.

Taya's eyes glistened. "Thanks. I needed this lunch more

than I realised. It's always so encouraging to sit down with the three of you and download everything going on in my life."

"I've been looking forward to this as well. Best part of my week."

"What are you going to do about that hole in the floor of your bookshop?" Bea asked before taking a bite of enchilada.

Evie sighed. "I don't know. Obviously I need to do a better fix than putting a big pot plant over it. I'm worried the pot will fall through the floor."

"Have you spoken to a contractor yet?"

"I've been meaning to get the number of the guy you used."

"Brett's good, and I'm sure he'll be able to help you out. I'll text you his details."

"Thank you."

"Do you want to replace the whole floor?" Penny asked.

"I'm thinking of doing an entire renovation. Bea already did that in the café, and it looks so good. When I walk into the bookshop after visiting her side, it looks dowdy and old."

"I love your bookshop," Bea objected. "It has character."

"It needs a little *less* character, if you ask me," Evie mumbled. "But thank you."

"Does this mean you're closing up shop for a while?" Taya asked. "I'm still recovering from the trauma of my own renovation at the inn."

"I suppose I'll have to, although I'm not sure what I'll do with myself."

"You could take a holiday," Penny suggested. "I highly recommend New Zealand. Rowan and I had such a wonderful time there—it's beautiful in a completely surprising way."

"Maybe," Evie replied. "I've never gone on holiday by myself. It's not nearly as much fun as going with someone else. That's why I haven't taken a trip in years."

"You could go on one of those organised tours that has a

whole bunch of single people on board a bus or something," Bea said around a mouthful of rice.

Evie couldn't imagine anything worse. A party bus full of young single people looking to get drunk and score. Nightmare. "I suppose, if I found a tour with people my own age."

"I'm sure you could," Penny said.

Suddenly Evie felt pathetic. It was the way her friends were looking at her, with pity and compassion in their eyes. She'd never seen herself as a sad sack before, but she was beginning to feel like one. She pushed a grin across her face. "I'll figure something out. Changing the subject—Bea, did anyone tell you about the secrets we uncovered while we were at your wedding reception?"

Taya and Penny exchanged a glance.

Bea frowned. "No. What are you talking about? What secrets?"

"Chaz and I were looking up Buck's pseudonym on my phone, and we stumbled across something interesting."

"We don't know anything for sure," Taya interjected.

"Right, of course," Evie agreed. "We don't know for sure, but we found an article — it was old and had been scanned into one of those websites that collects and organises newspaper clippings. Anyway, it talked about a woman who had kidnapped her son and was on the run. I did some more searching, and it turns out that this woman, Betsy Anne Gilmore-Alton, was still wanted by the police in California. They never found her or her son."

"The name Gilmore matches Buck's pseudonym, Samuel Jay Gilmore," Penny said. "That opens another can of worms I've never talked about — does that mean my last name is really Gilmore too, since he's my biological father?"

"I don't think so," Taya replied. "Your name is still your name."

"Maybe it's a coincidence that this Betsy shared the name

Gilmore," Bea replied, a crease between her brows. "It's not exactly a rare name."

"Could be," Evie replied. "It's worth looking into, although I'm not sure how we'd find anything more, since it was so long ago and happened on the other side of the world."

"There's one more thing," Taya said with a dip of her head. "We figured out that the mystery woman in those photographs from your cottage is Betsy. It has to be her. And the boy is her son. He doesn't look much like that cute little kid anymore, but I'm certain that was him."

Bea's expression grew serious. "I think you're right. I've seen photos of Betsy, and it certainly could be her. It's hard to say, of course, since the images are grainy and the film was so old when we processed it. But it makes a lot of sense."

"The only person missing from those photographs is my mother," Penny added. "So perhaps she took the photos when Betsy was in them, and then Betsy took them when Mum was posing. Who else could've been there?"

"I guess your mother would know." Bea cocked her head to one side. "You could ask her."

Penny groaned. "I can try, but I'm not sure I'll get much from her. She hates talking about anything to do with the murder. She pretends she doesn't remember and changes the subject most of the time."

"That's frustrating." Taya shook her head. "But understandable, I suppose. She doesn't want to be reminded of the pain she went through."

"There's a lot of shame around her relationship with Buck as well," Penny added. "For a long time, she wouldn't admit he was my father and didn't want to discuss anything about my parentage. Her lack of clarity on the topic has been an issue most of my life."

"It's all out in the open now," Bea said.

"And yet there are still so many secrets," Evie murmured.

Three

THE DRONE of music and gunfire was a constant reminder to Charmaine that her brother, Sean, was never going to leave. At least, that's how it felt. For weeks now, he'd lived with her in the tiny unit above the florist where she worked for Betsy. And he'd given no indication that he had any intention of leaving. The fact that he'd brought his PlayStation with him and had taken over her brand-new tiny television set, his legs splayed apart as he slouched in her bright blue bean bag while he shot bad guys, didn't help matters.

She sighed as she stirred a teaspoon of sugar into her cup of tea. "Any plans for the day?"

He shrugged and grunted.

She sighed again. "Maybe you should look for a place, find a job, get a ticket back to the mainland, disappear from my life never to be seen again?" She spoke beneath her breath, and he didn't respond. Likely he couldn't hear her over the drone of dance music repeating the same phrase over and over again. It was enough to drive any sane person mad.

"Please turn it down," she said, louder this time.

He reached for the remote and bumped the volume

button a couple of times. It made little difference, but it didn't matter anyway. She'd be late for work if she didn't leave soon. That was when she noticed the crumbs on the couch.

She strode to the piece of furniture and glared at it, as if it would provide some kind of answers for the state it was in.

"Did you eat on the couch again?"

"Huh?" Sean didn't break eye contact with the television screen.

"I asked you not to eat on the couch unless you're going to use a plate or tray. There are crumbs."

"Sorry," he mumbled with a grin. "I didn't realise you were such a fuddy-duddy."

"Fuddy-duddy?" She pressed her hands to her hips. "I don't want to encourage cockroaches and mice. That's all."

"Yes, Mum." He chuckled.

She fumed, her nostrils flaring. She wasn't being motherly. She was simply sick of him living in her unit, eating her food, and playing games on her television set. As nice as it was to have family around again, and she did enjoy his company, there was a line for how long a sister should support her older brother, and he'd most definitely crossed it. She was barely able to pay her bills on a good week, let alone with another hungry mouth to feed.

His brown hair flopped over his eyes, curls obscuring his vision. A dimple played in one cheek. He could be charming when he chose to be. Most of the time, it was hard for her to be angry at him — he was cute and fun, and he knew it. But today was not one of those times. Today, she was ready for him to get up off his lazy behind and find himself a job and a place to live.

But she couldn't say that because he was family. And not only that, but he was the last of her family. The only person in the world she was related to, other than the father she hadn't seen since she was tiny, so if he wanted to sleep on her couch forever, she would most likely let him. She couldn't bear the idea of breaking contact with him over something as trivial as personal space and couch crumbs. Still ... surely he would want to do *something* with his life before much more time passed. He'd never been one to sit still for long.

As she gathered dirty dishes and cups from the various places around the flat he'd deposited them, she drew in deep, calming breaths and reminded herself that this wouldn't last forever. He'd move on, the way he always did, and leave her wondering where he was and whether she'd ever see him again. It was Sean all over — no sense of boundaries, followed by no semblance of intimacy. Rinse and repeat.

"Remember when you told me about the solicitor and gave me that letter about Mum's will?" She'd been meaning to bring up their conversation so many times over the weeks, but hadn't been able to find an opportunity.

"Uh-huh," he said.

"Could you turn that off just for a minute, please?"

With an eye roll, Sean switched off the television and spun to face her. "You have my full and undivided attention, sis. What is it?"

She drew another deep breath. "I've been meaning to talk to you about Mum's estate. When I left town, they hadn't resolved her estate yet. You said you've spoken with the solicitor?"

Sean nodded, then strode to the kitchen to pour himself a coffee. "Yep. I wouldn't bother calling him, if I were you. You know about the house and the bank accounts. That's it, really."

Their mother hadn't been rich by any stretch of the imagination—Charmaine was well aware of that. But she had owned a small house, and in this market, even a small house was worth a decent amount of money. Especially when it was fully paid for, which she definitely recalled her mother doing, which was why she was confused.

They'd had a party that night — just the three of them. Mum had bought a mud cake from Coles, and they'd lit a candle and danced around, singing to the radio. Then she'd blown out the candle and shouted, "The house is finally mine, after all this time. I've scrimped, saved and paid off every single dollar. No more worrying about being thrown out by the bank. We might starve, but we'll always have a place to lay our heads."

There'd been tears in her eyes when she spoke. Even though Charmaine had been an adult at the time of the celebration, she hadn't fully understood until recently how much the achievement would've meant to her mother. Now that she was older and living at the mercy of a landlord, working minimum wage, she could comprehend the joy her mother must've felt after so many years of striving to provide for her children.

"I have questions about the house. Why was there so little equity left in it? I know Mum paid it off. Where did the money go?"

Sean shrugged. "She spent a lot of it before she died. She took out another mortgage. I'm sure you know more about it than I do. Didn't you rent it out?"

"One of Mum's friends rented it from me. I wasn't sure what to do since you skipped town and I couldn't sell it without your approval."

"You're right. I'm sorry—I should've been there."

"I don't get it." Charmaine shook her head. "Mum was so proud of herself for paying off that mortgage. Why would she get another one? And why not tell me about it?"

"She had a lot of bills. Especially after she got sick."

"She should've said something."

"You were dealing with enough—she didn't want to

burden you. Anyway, what does it matter now? The house helped pay for the two of you to live while she was sick, and it financed the treatments Medicare didn't cover. You've moved on. It's over."

"It would've been nice to know we had a little bit of money to fall back on after Mum's death."

"You seem to be doing pretty well on your own," he countered.

Charmaine bit back a retort. She wouldn't call bouncing from place to place for three years, living on minimum wage, never sure if she would be able to make her rent, doing well. But Sean didn't know what she'd been through. How could he? She'd never told him. As far as he knew, she had a nice, if somewhat cramped, unit close to the beach on a tropical island, with a decent job only a few steps from her front door. Things were good now. But there'd been a lot of heartache and anxiety along the way.

Maybe she wouldn't have left Newcastle right away if she'd had some equity in the house to draw from. Although, she hadn't been allowed to access any of her mother's accounts at first. The entire estate was frozen by the state after her death. It was standard procedure, Charmaine had been assured. But it didn't make things any easier for her, especially when the bills for the funeral took the last of her meagre savings. At the time, she couldn't believe that her mother hadn't done more to prepare for her passing.

Mum hadn't spoken to Charmaine about her estate or her last wishes. She hadn't handed Charmaine a sheet of paper with passwords on it for all her accounts, or a list of belongings and who they should go to. The only thing she'd discussed was that she wanted Charmaine to play the Carpenters at the funeral, and to scatter her ashes in the ocean off the coast of Newcastle.

Charmaine had done both things with a heavy heart.

Alone one evening on an empty beach as rain spattered against her face and a chill northeasterly did its best to foil her plans, she threw an urn full of ashes into the churning surf. It had been a frustrating ending to a horrible month for her, and all she'd wanted to do as she watched the waves take her mother's remains into their dark, roiling depths was to leave. To get out of there and not look back. To forget about it all and to start her life again, as someone else, in a new place.

"I suppose you're right. It wouldn't have changed anything. I only wish she'd told me. I thought I knew everything about her, but the more time passes, the more I learn about her. It's like I'm uncovering information about a stranger." She didn't like the way it made her feel. It was hard enough holding on to the memories that flitted like vapours in and out of her dreams some nights. To discover that her mother wasn't the open book she'd always seemed to be caused Charmaine's stomach to tighten. She shook off the encroaching nausea with a sigh and reached for her purse.

"I've got to go. We can talk more about this later."

As she shut the front door behind her, she saw her brother staring at the blank television screen. What was going through his head as he sat there? She wished she knew. It'd always been so difficult for her to read him, since his way of thinking was foreign to her own. Sometimes she'd imagine what he must be considering when he looked pensive and then he'd say something so unrelated or out of the blue, she'd realise all over again that he was the most unknowable person she'd ever met. And it scared her.

Four

AS THE LAST CUSTOMER LEFT, the bell above the door rang, and Evie exhaled a sigh of relief. It'd been a long day. She'd spent half of it showing the contractor around the bookshop and talking about floorboards, roofing, tiles and paint, and she'd had no time to eat or drink anything since she was the only one working the afternoon shift.

She finished counting the till, then closed her eyes and massaged her temples with her fingertips. The bell above the door rang again, and without opening her eyes, she declared, "We're closed."

"Surely you can stay open a little while longer," said a soft, feminine voice.

Evie's eyes blinked open, and her heart fell. She grimaced. "Emily."

Her sister was here. She'd been expecting this moment—dreading it. But she'd steeled herself to be positive, to be loving and kind. She hurried to embrace her twin sister, who laughed and flung her arms around Evie's middle, lifting her off the ground.

Evie groaned. "Put me down. We're the same size, and you'll hurt your back."

"I'm younger than you. Don't forget."

"Pffft ... by two minutes. That hardly counts."

Emily set Evie's feet back on the floor. Evie studied her sister. Her red hair had been bleached blonde and straightened. She was tanned and lithe, perhaps a little too skinny. Her cheeks were chiselled and her brown eyes darted from Evie's face to the door and back again. She'd always been a little skittish. Evie was the solid, reliable one. Emily was the artist who always seemed to have some kind of drama going on in her life. Drama Evie was glad to avoid.

"I wasn't expecting you yet," Evie said. "Mum mentioned you might come, but she didn't tell me a time."

"I had to get out of there. They hover. Have you ever noticed how much they hover?"

Evie laughed. "I've noticed."

"It's good to see you, sis."

"You as well." Evie hadn't been excited at the prospect of a visit from her sister when Mum first mentioned it, but now that she was here, she had to admit she liked it. They were twins, after all, and had a connection she couldn't deny. Even if Emily drove her crazy more often than not, she loved her above anyone else in the world. Besides, her mother had asked her to be nice, so she intended to try.

"My things are out in the car. Care to help me with them?"

Evie zipped up the cash bag with the day's take inside. "I've got to get over to the bank, but I'll give you my house key. There's no point bringing your things into the bookshop since I'm closing up."

"Isn't it a little early for that?" Emily's eyes narrowed. "Everything okay?"

"The customers are gone, and I have a throbbing headache. I'm closing early."

"Great. You can head home, and we'll catch up over a cup of tea. I'm dying to hear all about your life, since you never call anymore." She jabbed Evie softly in the ribs with her elbow.

Evie grimaced. "I call...I've been busy."

"Too busy to speak to your twin sister?"

"I'm sorry... you're right. I should call more often. I'm not good at the whole telephone relationship thing. Besides, you don't call either."

"That's why I'm here. We're both hopeless cases when it comes to staying in touch. We have to see each other more often."

Evie led Emily out of the bookshop, then locked the door behind them. She gave Emily the key to her house and watched as her sister drove away. It felt strange to lock her house, but Coral Island was changing. Or maybe it was only her perception that'd changed.

With a deep inhale of breath, she spun around to walk across the street to the bank. She'd deposit the money, then head back to the bookshop to finish up. It would be nice to go home early and spend time with Emily. She was curious to know what her sister was doing and why she'd moved in with their parents in recent weeks.

Back at the bookshop, she was about to step inside and pull the door shut behind her when a man's voice made her stop.

"I hope you're not closing up shop."

She turned to see the new primary school principal, David Ackerman, peering at her from the bottom step. He smiled, and a dimple appeared in one cheek.

"Sorry. I'm finished for the day."

He looked disappointed. "It's so hard for me to get over

here during business hours. I suppose I'll try again tomorrow."

He turned to leave.

She spoke up. "Come on in. Let's see if we can find what you're looking for. You can pay for it tomorrow, since I've already balanced the till."

He followed her inside, and she set the empty cash pouch by the register. "What can I help you with? Are you looking for a particular book?"

He shrugged and pushed his hands deep into the pockets of his dark jeans. "I don't know exactly. I've run out of things to read. Any suggestions?"

She strode towards the new release section with him in step behind her. "What genre do you like?"

"Anything fast paced. Action, I guess."

"I've got some brand-new books here that will be perfect for you."

She showed him each book, turning them over to read the blurb, while he watched her. He nodded and made sounds of agreement when she pushed one of the books into his hands, but he didn't seem particularly interested in it. It felt like he was there for some other reason.

"You know, we have a library in town."

He laughed. "Is this always how you do business? Try to get your customers to leave and find books elsewhere?"

Her cheeks flushed with warmth. "Of course not. But if we don't have what you're looking for..."

"I can go to the library. Got it. Thanks for letting me know. The truth is, I was hoping to see you again."

Warmth travelled from her neck up to her face, burning in her cheeks. "Oh?" She couldn't think of anything else to say.

He chewed his lower lip. "Uh... yeah. Well, I think I've embarrassed myself enough. But it was nice to see you. I'll bring the money for the book tomorrow."

"Wait," she said. It wasn't every day that a handsome single man came to Coral Island.

He stopped and faced her.

"Book club."

"I'm sorry?"

She swallowed. "Tomorrow night is my monthly book club. We hold it here at the shop at six o'clock. There's dinner and we talk about the book we've read the previous month."

"That sounds great. But I haven't read the book."

"It doesn't matter. Half the people there won't have read it either. But we still gather around a table loaded with food and wine and talk until the wee hours. It's fun—you should join us. If you want to."

His eyes lit up. "I'd love to. I'll see you then."

After he left, she shut the door and leaned against it, eyes closed. Then she exhaled slowly. How had it taken her this long to meet a man who was so handsome that he made her knees tremble, and with an interest in books? She'd spent much of her life single and alone. She'd missed the opportunity to raise a family. And *now* her Prince Charming had arrived? Better late than never, she supposed. She'd always wondered what it would be like to fall for someone the first time she met them. All she could think was how her quiet little life was about to be blown apart, and she wasn't sure how she felt about that.

* * *

By the time Evie had walked home, she was bathed in sweat and ready to get off her feet. When she opened the front door, she was glad to see that Emily had made herself at home, had switched on the AC, and was mixing margaritas in the kitchen, with Evie's apron tied firmly around her neat waist.

"You're an angel," Evie said, taking the glass she was

offered and leading the way into the living room, where she collapsed into her armchair. "Thank you."

"You're welcome. It's the least I could do. You work too hard."

"No, I don't. But my feet are aching and it's so hot today, I feel as though I've trekked through the fires of Mordor to get home, so this is perfect."

"You're such a nerd." Emily laughed, raising her glass. "Let's toast to nerds everywhere."

"Nerds everywhere," Evie agreed, clinking her cocktail against Emily's.

The drink was tart and icy. It was exactly what she needed. She lay her head back against the armchair, eyes closed for a moment as she enjoyed the flavour and coolness of it as it slid down her throat. Then, blinking, she studied her sister's profile.

"How are you?"

"I'm good." Emily sipped her drink.

"No, really. How are you?"

"I'm fine, honestly. I came here to see you. That's all."

"And what about your husband?"

"You know we've been having problems," Emily said with a toss of her head.

"True. The two of you are like a spark to a petrol spill." Evie ran a finger around the outside of her glass, watching the condensation part.

"We love hard, and we fight hard," Emily said with a sigh. "We needed some time apart."

"You've been staying with Mum and Dad..."

"Only for a few weeks. Before that, I was back home in Emerald."

"I know it's hard for you there."

"It's impossible. I can't stay. He's gone all the time — working in the mine or out with friends. He expects me to be fine on my own, but I don't have any friends. It's such a transient place, and most of the population is male. You know I've always gotten on well with men, but I'm married. I can't spend my time down at the local pub with a group of grubby miners while my husband is out doing who-knows-what with his mates. It's so frustrating — he doesn't listen to me. Says I don't do anything but complain." She smoothed her blonde hair back from her face with one hand and raised her glass to drink with the other.

"I'm sorry, sweetie." Evie's heart ached for her sister. She didn't realise how difficult it'd been on her in recent years. Her husband had worked for a mine for decades. He'd flown to central Queensland to work for ten days at a time, then came home again for ten days. They'd seemed to have a good life while they raised their two boys in Toowoomba, but now that the boys were out of the house, he wanted the two of them to be together. Apparently, Emily hadn't adjusted to her new life in the outback as well as it'd seemed from the outside.

Evie reached out to squeeze her sister's hand. They sat in silence for a minute as Evie battled to control her emotions while watching tears crawl down Emily's cheeks. She never could hold it together if her sister was hurting or upset. Finally, she set her drink down and moved to the couch to hug Emily.

They both overbalanced and landed on the arm of the couch. Evie tried to right herself, but her abs didn't work the way they used to, and she ended up looking like a turtle on its back. She gave up trying and instead squeezed her sister while choking back a giggle. After a few moments, Emily began to laugh through her tears as well.

"You haven't been doing your crunches," Emily sniffled.

"As I said, I've been busy." Evie finally smoothed her skirt over her legs. Then she returned to her armchair.

"I've missed you." A sentiment Evie never thought she'd

hear from her sister's lips. She'd have to apologise to Mum for doubting her.

"Me too," she whispered. She hadn't realised just how much until that moment. She'd held things against her for so long that she'd closed off her heart. But the truth was, she longed for her sister to be part of her life. She simply didn't trust her, and how could she let her back into her heart without trust?

Five

CHARMAINE WALKED ALONG THE STREET, a book tucked beneath her arm. A cool breeze whistled along the footpath, raising her hair from her neck and giving her goose bumps. She pulled her cardigan more tightly around her thin frame and shuffled closer to the dark shop fronts. She still wasn't used to the storms that sprang up out of nowhere and the wind that often buffeted the eastern-most parts of the island. However, tonight the wind had hit Kellyville on the western side of the island, and the sky was cloudless. Hopefully she'd be able to walk home from book club later without getting soaked to the bone.

The café was dark when she passed by the windows, apart from the faint glow of lights from the bookshop next door. She hurried around the corner to the bookshop's front door and pushed it open. The bell jangled above her head, and she looked up in surprise for a moment, her nerves making her forget that it always rang when she walked into the shop.

She shouldn't be nervous. It was silly to be scared of attending a book club. Readers were generally nice people—at least in her experience. But they were new to her and she was new to the club. She was always nervous when she went anywhere unfamiliar.

"Chaz, you made it!" Evie rushed to embrace her.

Charmaine blushed. "Thanks for inviting me. I've been looking forward to coming."

"We're glad to have you. The more the merrier. Come on in and get yourself a drink. Dinner is ready."

Charmaine made her way through the group to the drinks table. She couldn't believe how many people were there. Evie had suggested it was a small gathering and that she'd know everyone in attendance. But there had to be twenty people in the room, and to Charmaine's way of thinking, that wasn't small.

She reached for a glass and poured punch into it from a large bowl in the centre of the table with a ladle. Then she took a sip as she turned slowly to see who was there.

Bea sat in a chair against the wall, drinking a glass of wine and laughing with Taya and Penny. Bea's brother, Bradford, was there too. He was deep in conversation with a man she'd never seen before. Both men were tall and athletic. Bradford noticed her staring and offered her a wave.

Heat radiated up her neck and into her cheeks. She waved back and headed immediately for the empty chair beside Penny. She slid into it and continued sipping her drink for several seconds before Penny noticed her.

"Hi, Chaz. It's nice to see you," Penny said.

"Hi, Penny."

"I didn't know you were coming."

"Me neither, but I saw Evie a few days ago and she suggested it, so here I am. I didn't realise it was going to be so big."

"There's not much to do in Kellyville on a Wednesday night," Penny explained with a giggle.

Charmaine noticed a woman talking to several people on the other side of the room. She caught Charmaine's attention because her face was identical to Evie's, although more heavily made up. Her hair was blonde and straight, unlike Evie's red curls. But otherwise, she looked so much like Evie that if Charmaine hadn't already greeted Evie when she walked through the door, she would've sworn on her life that the blonde was Evie.

"Is that Evie? But I saw Evie earlier... Did she put on a wig since I arrived?"

Penny laughed. "It's Evie's twin sister, Emily. Uncanny, huh?"

"Evie has a twin sister?"

Taya spun in her seat. "Can you believe it? I haven't seen Emily in years. I wonder what she's doing here. Brace for impact!"

"What does that mean?" Charmaine frowned.

Bea spoke up. "Leave Emily alone. I'm sure she's changed. She's in her late forties—she can't possibly still be a wild child."

"Some things never change," Penny muttered beneath her breath. Then more loudly, she said, "I'm getting another glass of wine. Anyone?"

"I'll come," Taya called, raising her glass over her head and then hurrying off with Penny.

Bea slid into the seat beside Charmaine. "Isn't this fun? I'm definitely submerged in the island lifestyle if I'm excited about a book club, I know. But I do love it."

"I'm sure it will be fun. Only, I get a little nervous around strangers." Charmaine chewed on a fingernail. She wasn't sure why, but she always opened up more to Beatrice than she ever planned to. There was something about the older woman that enticed her to feel comfortable and safe. She almost couldn't help herself — the words simply tumbled from her mouth whenever Bea looked at her. Maybe it was the motherly aspect to Bea's personality.

Bea patted her on the leg. "You'll be fine. And anyway, most of us aren't strangers to you anymore. Are we?"

"No, you're right, of course. I should relax." She drew a deep breath into her lungs and forced her shoulders to lower, letting the tightness dissipate.

"I haven't seen you much lately."

"I've been busy. Sean moved in with me. Well, he says he's only visiting, but he's been living with me for weeks."

"Sean?" Bea's eyebrows flew up. "The brother you were hiding from? The one you said you were afraid to see?"

"Did I say that?" Charmaine crossed her arms over her chest. She knew she should've kept her private life to herself. It made her uncomfortable to know Bea had seen her vulnerability that way. Vulnerability always led to questions, and questions led to more opening up and before she knew it, she might be laid bare. The thought made her quiver inside.

"I don't know if you used those exact words, but it was implied." Bea looked concerned.

"Everything's fine. Sean needed a place to stay and I don't exactly have room, but he's crashing on my couch. I doubt he'll stick around. Coral Island isn't lively enough to keep him occupied for long."

"But you're okay?"

"Yes, I'm okay. I was wrong about him. I misinterpreted some things. But he's explained everything to me... well, he's *begun* explaining things to me, and I can see that I've jumped to some conclusions I shouldn't have. He's my brother so I have to give him a chance. Right? You'd give your brother a chance, wouldn't you?"

Charmaine glanced up at Bradford as she spoke the words, and her stomach tightened. Ever since she'd met him on the dock while he was fishing with his father and Bea's husband,

Aidan, she hadn't been able to stop thinking about him. He wasn't her type, not at all. She wasn't sure if she had a type, but if she did, it would probably be a man who was bookish and pale, like her. But Bradford wasn't either of those things. He was outdoorsy. Tall, broad-shouldered, and outgoing. She wasn't sure she could work up the courage to speak to him again, let alone spend time with him. She'd be better off if she could put him out of her mind. Although, being in a book club together was going to make that infinitely more difficult. She'd never have guessed he was a reader.

"I suppose you're right. I would give Brad another chance — he's my brother, and I love him."

"I love Sean too. We've been through a lot together."

"I'm glad you found each other. At least you know he's fine now." Bea offered her a look of compassion.

"Even though I was angry with him, there was this knot in my belly all the time when I thought about him. I didn't know if he was still alive. There's a sense of relief in knowing that he's here on the island with me, even if he is a pig to live with."

Bea snorted. "Aren't most brothers?"

Charmaine found herself laughing, her anxiety forgotten. "I don't know. I only have the one."

"Bradford isn't a good example, since he's a complete neat freak. But I don't think Sean is unusual in that regard. You seem happier, so that's a good thing."

"I am happier."

"Do you ladies mind if I join you?" Bradford appeared at Charmaine's side and pulled up a chair to sit between them.

"Not at all, Brad. I'm going to grab myself another drink. Chaz, can I get you anything?"

Charmaine still nursed her glass of punch. "No, thank you. Hi, Bradford." Her voice was soft.

"It's nice to see you again. Do you prefer Chaz or Charmaine?"

"I answer to either," she said. "But most people call me Chaz."

"You can call me Brad. I'm only Bradford when I'm in trouble."

"I can't imagine you'd ever be in trouble."

His eyes sparkled. "No, definitely not. I've always been perfectly well behaved. Didn't Bea tell you?"

Her pulse raced, and she felt a cold sweat break out across her forehead. The silence between them deepened.

Brad came to his feet with a grunt. "My drink's empty. It was nice to see you again."

As he wandered away, Charmaine resisted the urge to slap her forehead. He'd no doubt found her boring because she'd hardly said a word. Why didn't she say more? He was flirting with her and she'd clammed up, the way she always did. It was as though someone had stolen her tongue. Never mind—it was probably for the best. They could hardly have a relationship if she wasn't able to utter more than a few inane words in his presence.

He'd be better off with someone else, maybe Evie or her sister, after all he had to be at least ten years older than Charmaine, since he was Bea's younger brother. Charmaine was only twenty-six, which made Bea twenty years older than her. Perhaps Bradford was around forty. Not that it bothered Charmaine, to her age was only a number. But it did make him more suited to someone like Evie. And as far as Charmaine knew, they'd been friends forever. A relationship like that made sense.

The twins were beautiful, sophisticated, and currently engaged in two different, loud conversations with people she'd never met and probably never would meet because she couldn't bring herself to step outside her shell. Bradford was outgoing and warm, he'd suit one of them perfectly. She was mousy and awkward, found conversation difficult until she got to know someone well. How could she ever think he might be interested in someone like her?

Most of the time, her introversion was a warm, comfortable blanket she could curl up inside, protected from the world. But not tonight. Tonight it had let her down, and the frustration she felt made her stomach churn.

She meandered over to join the group around the table just as Evie announced it was time to eat. She peered between shoulders to see various salads and rolls with sandwich meats and cheese on several large platters. She took a plate, then filled a bread roll with ham and piled salad on the side.

Once her plate was full, she returned to her seat. The other ladies were back with plates of their own, and they all chatted amicably together while they ate. Evie joined them after a while, and Bea, Penny, and Taya all quizzed her about her sister. But she didn't say much—only that Emily was visiting for a little while because it'd been too long since they'd seen one another. Charmaine could tell that there was more to the story, but Evie wasn't going to divulge it while there were so many ears nearby straining to hear her words.

"Who's the man over by the door?" Taya asked. "Does anyone know?"

Evie pushed salad around with her fork. "That's David. He's the new principal at the primary school."

"Really? He's handsome," Penny said around a mouthful of bread roll.

"I hadn't noticed, but I suppose he is," Evie replied.

"*Sure* you didn't."

"I didn't." Evie shook her head. "Stop it."

"I'm not doing anything," Taya replied innocently.

Bea laughed. "It's nice to have someone new in town. This place gets a bit stale otherwise."

"Stale?" Taya frowned. "I don't think so. It's lovely the way nothing changes around here. Coral Island is the same as it was when we were kids, and it'll be the same when we're grandparents. There's something so reassuring about that."

"I suppose you're right," Bea said. "I'd be upset if it changed."

"Speaking of which, has anyone seen our favourite murderer out on bail yet?" Penny asked.

Bea's eyes widened. "That's some segue, Penelope."

Penny shrugged. "I'm curious. No one is talking about the fact that Buck is out on bail."

"I'm trying not to think about it," Bea replied. "But no, I haven't seen him. He's probably laying low. I doubt anyone is happy he's out—other than himself and Betsy, of course. Betsy is still so sure that he's innocent. I'm starting to wonder if we got it wrong as well."

Penny sighed. "I hope we're wrong. I really do."

Taya wound an arm around Penny's shoulders. "We all do, for your sake."

"Rowan doesn't want to talk about it," Penny continued. "I try to bring it up because sometimes there are things I want to get out in the open. Buck is his stepfather and my biological father, and he most likely killed my grandmother. That's a lot to process. But whenever I try to talk about it, Rowan changes the subject or uses some excuse to get angry with me and storm off."

"I'm sorry, sweetie," Taya said. "That's hard. But you can always talk to us if you need to."

"Definitely," Bea added.

"Absolutely," Charmaine agreed with a quick bob of the head.

"Thanks," Penny replied, her eyes glistening. "I know I can always count on you. Rowan and Buck have such a tortured relationship, it's hard for him to open up about it. I thought he was past all that, but then Buck got arrested. Now that he's out on bail, it's as though Rowan's in complete denial about the whole thing."

Once they finished eating, the book discussion began. Charmaine engaged in an easy back-and-forth with various members of the group and enjoyed herself far more than she'd thought possible when she first walked into the room. It was relaxed and lighthearted. There were some conflicts over which characters were the favourites and why, but it was all in fun. By the time it was over, she was excited about their next meeting.

When she stepped outside and waved goodbye to Bea, Penny, and Taya, she peered up at the moon for a few moments. The sky was dark and the moon was high in the sky — only a sliver. The crescent shone down on the inky water marking a trail.

"Beautiful night for a walk," Bradford said as he stepped outside.

"It's spectacular," she replied. "I love the smell of the ocean."

"Me too. There's something pretty special about it. Would you care to join me for a stroll around the dock?"

She looked at him in surprise. "Um… yes, okay."

They walked down to the dock in silence. Bradford's hands hung at his sides. Charmaine itched to slip her own hand into his, but didn't dare. Her heart thudded in her chest.

"Are you having a good week so far?" She almost cringed at her formality. Her words sounded hollow and empty in the beauty of the moment.

She wished she could see his eyes, but the darkness grew deeper as they moved closer to the shoreline. "It's been good. Busy, but satisfying."

"Work?" She asked.

He nodded. "It can get hectic at times. Which is positive, because it pays the bills."

43

"What do you do?"

"I run a yacht rental business out of Airlie Beach. We do deep sea fishing as well."

"That sounds like a great business to have in this area."

"It is," he replied. "And I love it. I get to be out on the water most days. Sometimes I'm stuck in the office doing paperwork, but I don't mind that either as long as it's not every day. How about you? How's the wedding planning business?"

"I haven't had any other weddings since your sister's, but I work at *Betsy's Florals* full time."

"I didn't realise that. Betsy's a lovely lady—I'm sure she'll take care of you."

"She's been amazing. She lets me live over the florist shop in exchange for me keeping an eye on the business, opening and closing each day—that kind of thing. Plus, she gave me a bike when I first arrived so I could get around the island. It was kind of her to think of me." She was babbling, but also somewhat in shock at how much she was talking. And it didn't feel awkward or scary. It felt natural and easy.

"You like to ride?" Bradford asked.

"I love it. I get to see the island close up, and it gives me some exercise. I'm kind of lazy, so if I had a car, I'd probably get very fat and never do anything active." She laughed. "Well, maybe I'm exaggerating since I do love to swim and snorkel, but I'm not the kind of person who'd get up early to go for a run every morning or play a team sport."

"I run every day," Bradford said. "And I'm on a Saturday soccer team."

She pressed a hand to her mouth. "I'm sorry. That wasn't a criticism."

He laughed and reached for her hand, cradling it in his. "Relax—I was just teasing you. I do run and play soccer, though. That wasn't a lie."

Fireworks ran from her fingers up her arm and hid in a ball in her belly. He was holding her hand and didn't seem to have any intention of letting it go. She bit down on her lip to keep from laughing out loud. Her nervousness often made her laugh at the most inappropriate times.

"So, I was thinking," Bradford began. "We should go out sometime. Maybe have dinner. What do you think?"

"I'd love that."

"Great, I'll give you a call."

"Okay."

He let their hands drop but didn't release his grip. His grasp was warm and gentle. His fingers linked with hers. They walked together around the dock and back again, talking quietly. He headed in the direction of her flat without mentioning it. Instead, he spoke about his work, his soccer team, the latest fishing trip. He asked about her life and family, questions she did her best to avoid answering directly. Then he stopped in front of the florist shop door.

"This is where you live. Right?"

He must've found out about her, she didn't recall telling him her address.

"Uh, yeah. How did you know?"

He laughed. "Don't worry, I'm not a stalker. I remember my sister saying something about it."

"I didn't think you were a stalker."

"Good to know." She couldn't see his expression well in the dim lighting of the street lamps but his voice was light-hearted and soft.

He pulled their hands to his mouth and kissed the back of hers gently, then released it.

"I'll see you soon, Chaz."

When he walked away, her heart hammered against her ribcage and she fumbled with her keys. What had just happened? She found it hard to believe any of what she'd experienced was real. Bradford Rushton, the tall, handsome, athletic businessman who every single woman in the island noticed, had escorted her home, kissed her hand and asked her out. She must be living in some kind of alternative universe. Things like that didn't happen to her — ever.

Six

THE COFFEE MACHINE BUZZED. Evie stood in front of it, staring at it, but not seeing it. Instead, her mind flitted between memories from the past she didn't often ponder. Having Emily come to stay had triggered images that rose up from the recesses of her mind unbidden. She and Emily dancing at the Tivoli together. Their parents so full of pride as they met them after the show with two matching bouquets of flowers — one yellow, one pink. As always. Or the time they went ice skating and Emily broke her ankle. She cried and Evie dried her tears and helped her from the rink. They'd been so close all those years ago.

They were a pair, always together. And now, they hardly spoke. It wasn't what Evie wanted — she longed for them to be close again like they used to be. But how could she trust Emily again after what she'd done? She could put the past behind her, forget her sister's actions, but trust wasn't so easily resolved.

How could she trust someone who had repeatedly betrayed her — the closest person to her in all the world, who hadn't stopped for a moment to consider Evie's feelings before

47

taking what she wanted over and over again? It was too much to bear. Wherever she went, Emily would show up — eager to reunite, acting as though nothing had gone wrong. And so eventually Evie had returned to Coral Island to hide away from her past. A place where she knew Emily wouldn't follow —there were too many ghosts living on the island for Emily's taste.

"Penny for your thoughts," Emily asked, poking her head through the back doorway.

"I was thinking about how much you hate this island. I'm surprised you've come."

Emily shrugged. "A lot of bad things happened, but it was an age ago. I almost can't remember it now."

"You mean Bea's mother?"

"And Penelope's grandmother. Not to mention my high school years — complete disaster. How did I manage to have so many friends turn against me in such a short period of time?"

"I plead the fifth," Evie replied with a grunt.

"You're not American."

Evie grinned. "I know."

Emily wiped her feet on the mat, walked inside with a handful of flowers from the garden. "These are beautiful. I didn't realise you were a gardener." She raised the flowers to her nose and inhaled their perfume.

"I'm an accidental gardener," Evie said as she poured milk into the two coffee-filled cups, then handed one to Emily.

"Accidental? What does that mean?"

"I was sitting on the back porch one day when I saw these wildflowers growing in the yard. I had an impulse to water them. Then I pulled the weeds from around them. Next thing I knew, I was building a garden bed and mulching. I thought I should add a few more so they didn't look so lonely... and here we are. I'm not sure what I'm doing, but I've read a couple of books, and so far it seems to be going okay. I haven't killed them all, at least."

"It's amazing." Emily searched cabinets until she found a vase, then filled it with water. "I love your house."

"It's tiny," Evie said with a grimace.

"Cozy," Emily countered.

They moved out to the back porch and sat in rocking chairs side by side while they sipped coffee.

Evie rocked herself slowly. "I'm sorry you're having such a hard time with your marriage."

Emily shrugged. "It's fine. We'll work it out. Or we won't. But either way, I'll be fine."

"You're calm these days."

"I've changed," Emily said. "I haven't seen you in so long, you've missed it."

"It takes two."

"I know it takes two, but you're the one with all the time. I've got a husband, two boys, and a life."

Anger churned in Evie's gut. It was always the same with Emily — she was the victim, and Evie was the selfish sister who didn't help. "I have a life."

"You know what I mean."

"Not really. You like to throw that in my face, as though not having a husband or kids means I don't have responsibilities. I have two businesses to run — and I'm making a living selling books and developing photographs. Do you know how hard that is?"

Emily raised her chin. "It doesn't sound difficult to me. More like fun."

"It's fun but sometimes I don't know how I'm going to pay the rent. And I don't have anyone to help me. No one to turn to when I'm running short of money. I have to do it all on my own. I know it's not the same as raising a family, but it has its challenges as well, and you never acknowledge that."

"You misunderstand me. I try so hard to get through to you, but all you can think about is yourself. You have no idea what I've been dealing with, and when I try to talk to you about it, you bring up your own hardships. You live in paradise, you get to do fun things with your friends all the time, you have a business of your own, and all you can do is complain." Tears pooled in her eyes and she spun on her heel to storm back into the house, slamming the door behind her.

Evie blinked, then set down her coffee cup on the small side table next to her rocking chair. She hadn't expected Emily to react that way, although her sister was often more dramatic than necessary. Still, was she right? Was Evie insensitive? She hadn't intended to be. But from her perspective, it seemed as though Emily always complained and never appreciated the difficulties in Evie's life. Perhaps they both felt that way — what was it about twins that they were always in competition with one another? It'd been like that for as long as she could remember. They'd been the best of friends up until high school, when competing for boys caused the first major rift between them. Although Emily had competed for their parents' love long before that.

With a sigh, she shuffled back into the kitchen. She needed to get out of the house. Perhaps she should go for a walk. She had taken the day off from work so she could spend time with Emily, and all she wanted to do was to get away from her.

Removing her straw hat from the peg by the front door, she stalked outside and down the footpath to the beach. When Emily was around, Evie felt as though the worst side of herself rose to the surface. With her friends — Taya, Bea, and Penny — she was happy, lighthearted, cheerful and easy-going. With Emily, she was selfish, snappy and insensitive. What was it about her sister that drew those qualities out from the darkest depths of her personality?

The mobile phone in the pocket of her denim overalls

rang. She pulled it out and was relieved to see Taya's name on the screen. She missed her friend so much when she travelled, and she'd left on the ferry that morning for a trip to Vanuatu.

"Taya, it's so lovely to hear from you. Everything okay?"

The sound of wind buffeting the microphone almost deafened Evie, and she pulled the phone away from her ear with a grimace. Then she put it on speaker.

"I'm fine. Calling to see how you're going. We didn't get a chance to talk last night. I'm on the ferry. Sorry, the wind is horrendous."

"Thanks for coming to book club, even though you were leaving so early this morning. It was good to see you."

"I loved it," Taya replied. "I didn't want to miss out on one of my favourite events with my favourite people just because of work. You did a great job with everything, by the way. But let's get down to the juicy stuff — why is your sister in town, and why didn't you tell me she was coming?"

Seagulls hovered overhead as Evie made her way along the beach, her sandals in one hand, the phone in the other. The sand was warm against her skin, and she dug her toes into its golden softness, leaning forward to stride through the the cove.

"I don't know exactly. We tried to talk about it a little bit — I think she's having some marriage difficulties."

"Oh, wow. I'm sorry to hear that. Although I'm tempted to say something about karma, I won't. I'll keep that to myself."

Evie laughed. "Don't go down that path. That's old news — we love Emily, remember? We want her marriage to work."

"I know. I'm trying to be supportive," Taya said. "My loyalty is to you, always."

"And I appreciate that. I truly do want only good things for her, yet for some reason, I can't seem to say that to her face and instead end up offending her and making her angry."

"I'm sure you were kind. You're always kind."

Evie shook her head even though Taya couldn't see. It wasn't true — when it came to Emily, she could be unkind. She never intended it, but there were things between them, things that'd happened in the past, that had built up resentment on both sides. Evie had tried to put it all behind her and move on, but some hurts were difficult to bury — they kept springing out of the sand all decayed and rotten and stinking up the place.

"I wasn't particularly kind, although I think she's a little too sensitive. But perhaps I should listen more and focus less on my own feelings. Do you think I'm selfish?"

"Definitely not selfish. You don't think of yourself often enough, in my opinion."

Taya was Evie's most loyal friend, but perhaps not completely objective in this instance. "When it comes to Emily, I mean. Am I selfish with my sister?"

Taya hesitated. "No, I don't think so."

"You paused. That means yes."

"No, it doesn't. I was considering your words, nothing more than that."

Evie slumped into the sand and rested her elbows against her bended knees to stare out across the ocean. "It's true, though. I'm selfish when I'm around my sister. She brings that out in me. I think it's because she's so ready to take, take, take that I feel as though I have to grab some things for myself before I miss out entirely."

"Those feelings are entirely justified, by the way. Given your history together."

"I suppose, but it all happened so long ago. She's been married for decades. They have two sons. What do I have?"

"You have a bookshop and your friends. You have a full life, Evie. Don't let this visit turn you upside down."

"I've got to go. I hope you have a great time in Vanuatu.

I'm completely jealous about all the food you'll be eating, and the amazing sights. I've always wanted to go there, so maybe send me a photo or something."

"I'll send you a selfie at the swim-up bar. But seriously, you should do all the things you've wanted to do, Evie. Don't let anything stop you from living the life you want."

"I don't want to do those things alone," Evie replied, her gut clenching with self-pity.

"You don't have to — I'm here."

"You've got Andrew. Forget it, I'm being melodramatic. Of *course* we can go somewhere together. As soon as I've paid for all these renovations I'm planning."

"Things aren't so bad as they seem, honey. You're going to be okay." Taya's voice was soothing, but Evie heard a hint of worry in her tone.

"I'm fine—really, I am. I was having a moment, but it's passed, and now I'm going to eat some breakfast and get on with my day. Thanks for calling."

"Talk to her," Taya said. "I know she means a lot to you, and I hate to see you struggle so much with this relationship. Talk to her and get some things out in the open that you've both avoided discussing for far too long. It'll be emotional and it might hurt, but you've got to do it."

Evie hung up the phone and squeezed her eyes shut as two tears trailed down her cheeks. Then she shoved the phone into her pocket, and strode for home.

Seven

EVER SINCE BRADFORD asked her out, Charmaine could hardly think about anything else. She'd be trimming flowers and her heart would flutter against her ribcage as an image of his face drifted across her mind's eye. Or she'd be out walking, taking photographs to paint with watercolours later in her cramped flat, when she'd see a man in the distance who reminded her of him, and her cheeks would flood with heat in an instant.

He'd suggested they have dinner together, but he hadn't called her yet. So far, her phone had been silent apart from the occasional text messages Sean sent her throughout the day, driving her mad.

Her brother still hadn't found a job or a place to live, much to her dismay. She picked up a broom and began sweeping the florist shop. Betsy had stepped out to collect Samantha from school. They would be back soon, and Charmaine wanted the shop to be sparkling clean for them when they arrived. Betsy had seemed a little down lately, and Charmaine was doing whatever she could to perk her up.

She swept all of the leaves, stems and petals into a pile and then threw it in the bin. Just as she was bending over to pick up the dustpan, something in her back tweaked. She froze in place with a squeal, then hobbled over to the nearest chair to sit. Even the act of sitting was painful. She grimaced and rubbed the base of her back as best she could. This was no good — it'd happened before. Apparently, she had a bulging disc or something. She'd seen a chiropractor a year earlier about it, but that had only made the pain worse. So, she'd given up on treating the issue and instead had focused on ignoring it. The approach had worked well until today.

After sitting still for a few moments, she shifted to the floor and began stretching out her lower back by holding one leg across her body and then the other. Before long, she managed to stand and straighten her back as Betsy and Sam walked into the shop.

"Hi, Chaz," Sam called out as she ran past Charmaine and headed for the small refrigerator in the kitchen behind the shop. Betsy kept it stocked with all of the treats Samantha loved. Chaz had been worried when Sam hadn't come to the shop for several weeks, but she'd started back with the routine without a word about her absence. Charmaine hadn't commented, and everything seemed to be back to normal.

When she'd asked Betsy about it later, the grandmother had simply mumbled something about much-needed time off — perhaps Sam and her father had gone on a holiday together. But the absence had started after an altercation between Sam's dad and Betsy, when he yelled something about her being a liar and a fraud. The conflict was more likely to be the reason that Sam hadn't come around much for a while. But it seemed they'd put the rift behind them, since Samantha had spent every afternoon that week at the florist shop with Charmaine and Betsy.

She soon returned without her school backpack, licking a chocolate-covered ice cream.

"How was your day?" Charmaine asked, continuing to stretch, this time focusing on her legs.

"It was fine."

"Is your back playing up?" Betsy asked as she reached for the glasses hanging around her neck and slipped them onto the bridge of her nose. Her grey hair hung around her face in beach-style waves, and she wore an aqua silk kaftan with large pink flowers on it.

"It seized up for a few minutes, but I think I've worked out most of the kinks."

"You should take something."

"I would, but everything is upstairs and I'm not sure I can climb..."

"I've got something in the first aid kit. I'll get it for you." Betsy disappeared through the back door and then returned with two pills, which she handed to Charmaine with a glass of water. "Drink up."

"Thanks, Betsy. You're a life saver."

"Can't have you limping around here in pain, can we?"

Charmaine took the pills then returned the glass to the kitchen. She felt strangely emotional about the exchange. Betsy wasn't exactly the warm and fuzzy type. She was a strong, resilient woman who rarely showed how she was feeling. But her stoic form of affection was to do things for people — to serve them in the way they needed to be served. And it warmed Charmaine to have someone care for her. It'd been a long time since she'd had that with her own mother, and now Betsy had become something of a grandmotherly figure to her.

"You haven't been outside all day. You should get a coffee, relax and enjoy the day a little while," Betsy recommended. "I'll watch the shop for a couple of hours. You can close up when you get back. It's not likely to be busy."

"Really? That would be nice. I forgot to eat lunch, since we had that big order to fill. I think I'll pop over to *Bea's Coffee* and get something to eat."

She took off her apron and smoothed her hair in the mirror. A painting hanging on the wall beside the mirror caught her eye. It was by a local artist. The entire florist shop was covered in paintings by artists. Betsy offered the space to them so they could sell pieces and it made the shop looked nice. It was a good strategy and worked well. Perhaps she should ask Betsy if she could hang some of her own artwork. She'd never sold anything before, but she'd been getting more serious lately — painting almost every night. Her television set was completely dominated by Sean's game playing, so she'd had to occupy her evenings in other ways. Painting and reading were her favourite pastimes.

This painting, however, spoke to her. It was a seascape with some children playing on the beach. It was painted in an impressionist style, and the colours were eye-catching. It touched something deep inside of her, made her feel. That was what great art was supposed to do, and this painting did that for her. She glanced at the artist's name.

Finn Edgeley

Finn... that name was familiar. Suddenly she recalled the name on Watson's collar. Her wandering cat's real owner was a Finn. Perhaps it was the same person. It seemed too coincidental to be anything else. Surely there couldn't be too many Finns in a town as small as Kellyville.

"Do you know this artist?"

Betsy squinted at the painting. "Oh, sure, Finn. She paints a lovely seascape."

"She's a woman?"

"Last time I looked." Betsy laughed. "Why?"

"No reason. I presumed Finn was a man's name. Is she the same person who owns Watson, my cat?"

Betsy cocked her head to one side. "Um... yes, I think that's right. I'm not up on all the pet owners around here. Pets aren't my thing. But yes, pretty sure she's the one who owns the cat, although everyone in the street feeds him. He's going to get very chunky one day."

Suddenly Charmaine had an intense desire to meet this woman. She had a fantastic cat, who she happened to be completely fine about sharing with the entire neighbourhood. And she was an amazing artist who had managed to capture the seaside surrounding Coral Island in a way that Charmaine had been attempting to do for months. She must be an interesting woman.

"You know, you should hang some of your paintings up around the shop," Betsy said. "You're a talented painter yourself."

"Really? Thanks, Betsy. That would be amazing." Charmaine's stomach did flips as she thought about hanging her own artwork up for people to critique or perhaps buy. It was exciting and scary in equal measure.

Betsy looked at her in a loving kind of way that Charmaine hadn't seen before. "You came along at just the right time, Chaz. I can't tell you how much I needed you. So, you should treat this place like your own. Put your paintings on the walls, think about how you might like to improve things—whatever would make you most comfortable. I'm open to any and all suggestions."

Charmaine's heart swelled. "Thanks, Betsy. I love working here. You basically saved my life." There was no way for her to express how much she appreciated all Betsy had done for her. She'd taken her in, a stranger off the street with nothing more than a backpack and a sad story. Betsy had given her a job, a place to live. She'd believed in her, trusted her, and opened up a whole new world to a woman who'd come close to giving up on ever finding love, connection or family again.

Betsy dabbed at her eyes. "Well, get out of here then, and enjoy yourself. You can't work all the time. You're too young for that."

"Okay, I'll see you in a while," Charmaine said as she headed for the door. What would've become of her if she hadn't felt the urge to walk into the florist shop that day? She didn't know, and she didn't want to. Her life had turned around the moment Betsy said yes to giving her a job. She would be forever grateful to the older woman.

She tried to imagine her itinerant life and where it might've taken her if she hadn't met Betsy that day. But she couldn't stop thinking about Finn and her cat. Watson's grey face kept sliding across her imagination. He'd purr then lick his chops.

The fact that the artist whose paintings she'd so admired since she arrived might be her cat's true owner was something she couldn't get out of her head. If she wanted to meet Finn, all she had to do was call. After all, she'd texted her right after Watson first spent time in her flat to let her know where her cat was, so she had her phone number. But wouldn't it be strange for her to call a woman out of the blue who she'd never met? The introvert in her shrank from the idea.

The street was almost empty. Most of the tourists had left for the day. But before she reached Bea's Coffee, she noticed Penny on the footpath ahead, talking to a man. At first she didn't recognise him, but then his face triggered a memory from a newspaper article she'd read. It was Buck Clements—she was sure of it. She dodged into an alleyway and pressed herself up to the brick wall of the Thai restaurant. She was close enough to overhear their conversation.

"What do you want?" Penny asked, her voice frosty.

"I want to see you, to talk to you." Buck had a tinge of an American accent, and his tone was gruff.

"We have nothing to talk about. You killed my grandmother."

"It's not true, none of it. I didn't kill her. Why *would* I kill her? It makes no sense."

"Maybe she threatened to tell the police about you and my mother."

"Why would she do that? I didn't do anything illegal. The age of consent was sixteen."

"What you did was wrong. She was a child."

"I know it was wrong. I didn't realise it at the time, but I've regretted it ever since. I shouldn't have done it. I was lonely. You don't know what it's like to come to a foreign country and leave behind everyone you know and love. I felt so out of place, so disconnected from everyone and everything. You've lived on the island all your life—you don't understand what being an outsider feels like."

"You had your sister and your nephew."

Charmaine couldn't see his reaction, but she heard a grunt. "I suppose that's true, but it's not the same. You don't know the whole story."

"I don't want to know the whole story. At least, I'm not sure I do. I want to believe you're innocent, but the evidence says otherwise."

"Does it?" he asked. "I don't think so. I think people have twisted the evidence to make it seem like I'm guilty because they wanted a patsy. But the police never pinned this thing on me all those years ago, and they've all but admitted they don't have the evidence now. I'm sure they'll find a way to put me behind bars anyhow, but it won't be right. It'll be to appease the community, nothing more."

"Who is Samuel Gilmore?"

Buck hesitated. His voice was quieter when he spoke. "That was me, a long time ago."

"Why did you change your name? What are you running from?" Penny's voice trembled.

"I came here to support Betsy. She was alone with her son. I wanted a fresh start. That's all there is to it. You wouldn't understand. And this isn't the time or place..."

"If you didn't kill my grandmother, who did?"

Charmaine peeped around the corner to see Buck shrug. He crossed his arms over his broad chest. "Don't give up on me. That's all I'm saying."

"I don't *know* you," Penny objected, but her tone had softened.

"That's my fault."

"Why didn't you ever try to find me, to talk to me?"

"Your mother didn't want me to. She said it would confuse you, and after the way things worked out, I don't blame her. She thought I was a murderer. She didn't want anything to do with me."

"And after she left the island?" Penny's voice rose in pitch.

"By that time, it was too late. I didn't think you'd want to know me, and I convinced myself we were both better off keeping things the way they were. I shouldn't rock the boat. I saw you every now and then—seemed to me you'd built a good life for yourself. I'm proud of what you've done, putting together that animal refuge. It's really something."

"Thank you." Penny hesitated and swiped at her cheek with one sleeve. "But I wanted to know my father. All my life, I've longed to know you. I asked Mum over and over about you, but she lied and said you were gone. It could've been different. There's been fallout: I don't know how to love. I'm married, but it's hard to accept intimacy from a man because I was rejected by you for so long. You've messed me up—do you know that?" She sniffled and wiped her nose with her sleeve again.

Charmaine's heart ached for Penny. If only she could give

her a hug. But she wasn't supposed to be listening in on this conversation. Perhaps she should try to sneak away, but it wasn't likely she could do that without being seen.

"What can I do to make things better?" Buck let his hands fall to his sides, fists curled and yet impotent.

"Nothing. There's nothing you can do. I need time to think." Penny sighed, then walked away, leaving Buck standing alone in the street.

He glanced at Charmaine, meeting her gaze for a single moment with a pained expression, then he strode off in the other direction. After a few moments, Charmaine stepped out from her hiding place. She shouldn't have listened, but she didn't want to embarrass Penny by walking past. And now she'd overheard a private conversation. Somehow Charmaine had missed the fact that Betsy's criminal brother was also Penny's father. This town was so confusing at times. Just when she thought she was getting a handle on how everyone was connected, something like this happened to push her off balance all over again.

She hurried to Bea's café and found a table at one of the windows that looked out on the street. She wasn't sure where Penny had gone, but maybe she'd see her if she walked by and she could say something — but what could she say to comfort her new friend after an exchange like that? She didn't know, but she wanted to be there for Penny the way Penny had been for her since she arrived on the island.

"Hey, Chaz. Can I get you something?" Bea held a pencil poised above a small notepad.

"I'd love a Caesar salad and a smoothie, please."

"How are you? You look a little pale. Have you been working too hard again?"

"I'm fine. A little hungry, that's all."

"Well, I'll get that order in and you'll be eating in no time. You've got to take care of yourself, you know."

"I know. Thanks, Bea. Hey, quick question..."

Bea leaned on the table. "What is it?"

"Have you seen Brad lately?"

"He's right over there." Bea pointed across the café to where Bradford sat at a table with his laptop in front of him. Shoulders slightly hunched, he leaned forward and tapped at the keyboard. The computer looked tiny next to him, and the chair much too small for him. An empty coffee cup sat on the table beside the laptop.

"Okay. Thanks."

Bea left to get the food, and Charmaine sat watching Brad with her stomach churning. Should she go over and say hello? But what if he wanted some privacy? He looked to be working —she shouldn't interrupt him. She could talk to him the next time she saw him, when he wasn't busy.

He looked up and caught her eye. A broad smile crept across his face. He picked up the laptop and headed her way.

"Hi, Chaz. Good to see you. Can I join you?"

She nodded.

He sat and closed his laptop. "Sorry I haven't called."

"It's okay," she said. "I'm sure you've been busy."

"No, that's not it... I *have* been busy, but actually I dropped my phone in the ocean. I was out on one of my yachts, and it slipped out of my pocket. It was as if everything was moving in slow motion, but I couldn't get to it fast enough, and plop, into the water it went." He laughed. "It wasn't funny at the time, but I can joke about it now."

"Wow, I'm sorry. That's so annoying." At least he had a good excuse for not calling her. Suddenly she felt much better about the whole thing.

"Very annoying. Especially since I lost all my numbers. But they're backed up in the cloud or something, so they assure me that when I pick up my new phone this afternoon, it'll have all the numbers restored on it. I'll finally be able to call you and ask you on that date."

"I'm looking forward to it," she said shyly.

Bea set Charmaine's salad plate on the table, along with her smoothie. "Here you go. Enjoy!" She offered Brad a wink.

"You're eating?" Brad asked. "I should order something too and we can eat together. It can be our pre-date. Is that okay? Or am I stepping on your plans?" He arched an eyebrow.

"It's a great idea," she said. "I have no plans. I was going to eat alone and now I don't have to."

He grinned. "Perfect. I'll be right back."

She watched him jog over to the counter and order food from Bea. He laughed with his sister over something on the menu. His brown hair was wavy and thick. His tan was dark in contrast to his white T-shirt.

What was she doing? He was exactly the kind of man who had never paid her any attention before. And for the life of her, she couldn't understand why he'd asked her out. They were polar opposites. How could it possibly work out between the two of them?

He strode back to the table and sat across from her.

"How's your week been?" He asked.

She set her fork down. She should wait for his meal to arrive. "It's been fine. How about you?"

"Please, go ahead and eat. Mine will be here soon, but you must be hungry. I don't want to hold you up."

"I don't mind," she said, as her stomach grumbled.

"I insist. I can talk while you eat."

And so he did. He talked about himself, his family, his childhood on the island. How much he loved snorkelling and soccer. And she got to know him, slowly but surely, seeing the man behind the attractive facade.

His food arrived and he sliced off a piece of chicken

parmesan, popping it into his mouth with a sigh. "Bea's parmi is the best."

"It must've been great to have a sister like her. I've always wanted a sister."

"You only have a brother. Right?" Bradford asked.

She nodded. "He's staying with me at the moment."

"What's his name again?"

"Sean," she replied.

"And how's it going with Sean and you in that tiny flat?" He grinned.

She grimaced. "Let's just say he spends all day on his Playstation, and I'm probably going to find dirty dishes and discarded underwear all over the place when I go home."

He grunted. "Sounds like a nightmare."

"One I'm not likely to ever wake up from," she confirmed.

"He's staying?"

Her lips pressed together into a straight line. "It seems that way."

"Can't you kick him out?" Bradford scooped up some salad with his fork and munched on it.

"He's family," she said.

"I'm sorry," he replied. "I know family can be tough."

"It's okay," she said. "I'm glad I ran into you. Gives me a chance to forget all about my wayward brother for a little while."

They talked for two hours before Charmaine realised it. The time passed quickly while the two of them had a slice of pie for dessert followed by a leisurely coffee. Finally, Bradford left to attend a business meeting on the mainland. Charmaine stretched her legs, which were cramped from sitting in the same place for so long. Then wandered to the register to pay.

"Already paid for," Beatrice said, with a smile. "Have a great day."

Charmaine walked out into the sunshine with a giddy

feeling bubbling deep down in her gut. It was amazing how quickly things could turn around. She'd started the day in a foul mood, with no hope that things would improve. And now all she could think about was how bright the future looked from where she stood.

Eight

FROM THE MOMENT the renovation on the bookshop began, everything went wrong. They ordered the wrong-sized support beams to redo the ceilings. The paint came in charcoal when it was supposed to be a light grey. The floorboards were rotten in so many places, they had to redo the entire thing, and the wait time for the order was going to set them back weeks.

Already Evie was more stressed than she'd been in years. And having Emily around only exacerbated those feelings.

"I opened a bookshop because I don't like stress," she said, tucking a pencil behind one ear as she studied the plans laid out on the small folding table. "I dreamed that selling people books would involve me sitting with my feet up in a soft armchair, reading while customers quietly browsed through the shelves. I was completely delusional, but that's beside the point.

"I don't like feeling pressed in on all sides and that's all I've had lately — complaining customers, damaged books, stubborn suppliers and disgruntled tourists. Not to mention the building falling down around me and the landlord ignoring my requests for help. I get cheap rent, she said, so the fine print on the contract is that any upgrades are my responsibility. I can't believe I signed something like that without running it past a lawyer. Of course, at the time I'd sunk all of my capital into stock and didn't have a cent to spare on legal fees. This is all so frustrating!"

"You never handled pressure well," Emily muttered as she tapped the lids of the paint cans back into place with the end of a screwdriver. "You always say I'm a complainer, but wow..."

"That's not helpful right now," Evie growled. "Maybe you could take the cans outside to wait for the delivery driver."

Emily sniffed. "I didn't come here to be free labour for you."

"You're a grouch. Did anyone ever tell you that?"

"I thought I'd be lazing on the beach and soaking up the sunshine," Emily said as she picked up one can in each hand and headed for the door. "Instead, I'm your errand girl."

"Nothing you don't deserve," Evie muttered beneath her breath.

Brett O'Hanley, the builder she'd hired to do the renovation appeared suddenly behind her. "Huh? Did you say something?"

"No, nothing important. So, when do you think we can get started on the floorboards?"

"Not for weeks yet. The manufacturer is in China, and there's a backlog. Nothing we can do about it, I'm afraid."

"So, I won't be back in business for months?"

"We'll put some temporary flooring down to keep people from falling through the holes. You can reopen if you don't mind the way it looks."

She sighed. "I can live with that. Thanks, Brett."

Voices outside caught her attention. Maybe the delivery driver had returned to collect the paint. She wanted to speak to him, to remind him to check the labels on the cans for the correct colour number before he came back. She had painters standing around, on her dime, with nothing to do until the order was filled correctly. It made her skin crawl to think of her bank account rapidly shrinking with every passing moment.

She tiptoed around the holes in the floor to the front door and looked out the gap to see David talking to her sister on the landing. Emily pushed her blonde hair behind one ear and looked up at him with a flirtatious smile.

"I love the blonde," he said. "Makes you look younger."

"Thanks. I feel younger," Emily said.

Evie frowned. Perhaps they'd met at book club the other night, although she hadn't seen them connect. Emily had spent most of the night hiding in a back corner talking to another one of the men in attendance.

"Have you lived on the island a long time?" he asked.

She shrugged. "I grew up here, but only returned recently."

"Oh? It must've been wonderful to spend your childhood somewhere so beautiful."

"It was. We ran around in bare feet and bikinis for most of the year."

"What a fantastic childhood. I'm afraid I was raised in the city. I spent a good portion of each day catching the train to and from school with a million other people, all of us jammed into the carriages like sardines."

"I had a pretty special upbringing. Sometimes I wish I could go back to being a kid all over again."

"I understand that," David replied, leaning against the railing. "I see these kids at the primary school who seem as though they don't have a care in the world."

"Being an adult is hard," Emily said.

David laughed. "The thing is, I didn't love my childhood. So, I'm enjoying adulthood. It's a much better time for me. I can do the things I've always wanted to do. And I can help other kids have the kind of school experience I didn't have."

"That's so noble," Emily replied, batting her eyelashes. "You're a good man."

Evie cringed. Her sister could be corny when she was flirting. She'd be angry if she wasn't so used to it. They were much older but in many ways, nothing had changed since they lived together all those years ago.

"Evie, I was wondering if perhaps you'd like to go on a date with me this Friday."

Evie's eyes widened. He'd come to the bookshop after school to ask her out on a date, and instead he'd seen Emily on the front porch and assumed she was Evie?

Emily laughed and pressed a hand to David's arm. "I'd love to go out with you, but my name is Emily."

Confusion flitted across his handsome face. His brown eyes looked troubled. "I'm so sorry. I thought you said Evie, and I'm usually pretty good with names."

"It's fine," she replied. "She's my twin sister." She held out a chunk of her hair. "Blonde, not red."

He gaped. "Oh, wow, of course. I should've realised that. I thought she'd coloured her hair."

"What's your name again?"

"David," he replied. "It's nice to meet you, Emily."

"And you as well, David. Friday night sounds wonderful. Does seven o'clock work?"

He cleared his throat, gaze darting to the bookshop door. "I, uh..."

If she were more vindictive, Evie would've stepped outside and told David her sister was married. She'd noticed Emily wasn't wearing her wedding ring these days. Perhaps their marriage was over, and she simply didn't want to admit it. Regardless, Evie didn't have the strength to bother making a fuss. If David wanted to go on a date with Emily, she wouldn't stand in the way. She'd done enough fighting with her sister over men in the past—she never intended to do it again.

"I'll see you then, David," Emily said, pressing her hand to David's chest and smiling up at him.

His cheeks flushed red and with a stammered agreement, he hurried down the stairs and back in the direction of the school.

Evie stepped outside and crossed her arms. She glared at Emily.

"What?" Emily poked out her chin.

"He came over here to ask me out..."

"But he didn't. He asked me instead."

"You're married."

"It's dinner. Don't be a prude."

Evie shook her head. "Why did you come, Em? You don't seem to be here to see me."

"Of course I am. I love you—you're my sister. And there's nothing wrong with having a little fun at the same time. You know me. I can't stand to be boring."

"There's definitely nothing boring about you. I'll have it engraved on your headstone — Emily Mair was self-centred and cruel, but she was never boring," Evie said before slamming the door shut behind her and striding across the bookshop.

Brett looked up from his work measuring the space, surprised at the loud noise. "Everything okay?"

"Do you have siblings, Brett?"

"Two brothers," he replied with a nod, his grey moustache twitching.

"Then you get it — they can push your buttons like no one else."

He chuckled. "You're right about that."

Evie stopped in the small kitchen behind the shop and leaned against the bench, eyes shut. She groaned and rubbed both hands over her face. It didn't matter to her who David dated. He was an adult—he could go out with anyone of his choosing. But the fact that Emily had once again gotten in the way of Evie's life, her friendships and relationships, grated on her last nerve. She'd thought the pain of the past was well and truly behind her, but it stoked a fire of anger in her gut.

She'd walked away—no, she'd *run* would be a more apt description. She'd run back home to Coral Island to get away from the wounds her sister had inflicted on her years earlier. And now that Emily was back, Evie felt as though she were thirty-eight years old all over again, having her heart torn from her chest. Perhaps she hadn't put the past behind her so much as she'd hidden from it, and now the feelings she'd buried were working their way to the surface to haunt her all over again.

Nine

IT'D BEEN a rough day at work. The only redeeming feature was that Charmaine had hung two of her paintings in the florist shop and several customers had stopped to look at them. One had remarked on how lovely the painting was. No buyers yet, but she was happy with the initial response to her artwork, given that she hadn't shown it off to anyone before.

Now, however, Charmaine wanted nothing more than to lie down on the couch and vegetate in front of the television set. But Sean would be there. He was always there. And he'd be waiting for her to cook dinner for the two of them so he could watch Friday night football. She'd have to watch with him or be relegated to reading on her bed.

She should stand up to him—it was her flat, after all. But she couldn't bring herself to do it. Conflict was something she did her best to avoid. She didn't like talking to strangers, avoided gatherings as much as possible, and hated to get into any kind of disagreement.

She'd once let her hair grow down past her waist because she didn't want to argue with her hairdresser, who'd insisted she needed layers and a fringe when she didn't want them.

Instead, she'd simply avoided going to the hairdresser at all for five years until the woman had resigned and moved on. She could've found another hairdresser, but then she was afraid she'd have to explain if she ever ran into the lady at the grocery shop on the corner between her house and the hairdresser's, and she didn't want to change where she shopped.

It was exhausting being her at times. But she supposed there was nothing to be done about that.

She'd closed up the florist shop late because Betsy had left her filling an order that she said she'd come back and collect to deliver later that night. But she'd wanted to take Sam home to see her father, since he had car troubles of some kind and couldn't pick her up. Charmaine had stayed behind, snipping stems and arranging flowers, tying them together into beautiful arrangements, for a wedding happening at the *Blue Shoal Inn* the next morning.

Weddings were her favourite event to decorate with flower arrangements. She used all her creative energy to make them as beautiful as possible. Betsy had spent hours training her over the months since she arrived. Charmaine became more confident with every job she undertook.

She'd also been hired to plan several weddings since Bea's, and she seemed to be making a bit of a name for herself on the island as the only available wedding planner. She enjoyed every minute of it now that she'd figured out a few ways to streamline the process. The first weddings she'd planned had given her repeated panic attacks, but now she knew what she was doing — at least, much better than she had. And she was confident in helping her brides with their dream weddings.

In fact, she should go upstairs and finish the presentation she was preparing for her next meeting with a bride from Airlie Beach who was planning for her upcoming nuptials on the island. The theme was bikini chic, although Charmaine wasn't sure you could ever call a bikini wedding *chic*. Still, she was doing her best to make the woman's dreams come true and already had some great ideas on how to create a few special moments that would bring the whole thing together beautifully.

When she pushed her way into the flat, the first thing she noticed was the state of the small kitchen. The sink was full of dirty pots, pans and dishes. There was some kind of burned food smell hanging in the air, combined with the stench of a full litter box. The same litter box Sean had promised to empty that morning, but that Charmaine could clearly see was still just as full as it had been then.

She spun around slowly, taking in the disaster that was her previously neat and tidy flat.

Sean's bedding lay crumpled on the couch, formed in the shape of his body from the last time he'd sat there, playing video games. There were chip crumbs surrounding the body-sized hole in the doona, along with a few splashes of salsa. There was some kind of stain on the coffee table, where something hadn't been wiped up in time. And dirt from a large pair of boots was trekked across the floor from the back door.

Her nostrils flared as she scanned the room looking for her brother. It was time she let him know how she felt about his housekeeping efforts. She couldn't kick him out—he was family. But the least he could do was show his gratitude by helping out around the tiny flat. It wasn't as though there was a lot of work to do in such a small space, but he didn't attempt any of it, and hadn't from the moment he'd arrived. He'd always been a self-centred boy, but she'd expected he would grow out of that phase eventually, especially after their mother died three years earlier and the two of them had no one to take care of them. But apparently Sean had managed to avoid growing into maturity while living on his own.

He wasn't in his usual places—in the kitchen, standing in

the open door of the refrigerator eating her food, or hunched in front of the television set. Where was he?

Rustling came from the linen closet around the corner from the kitchen. She tiptoed over, hoping she wouldn't find a rodent or something equally disgusting getting into food remnants that her brother had no doubt left scattered across the floor. When she poked her head around the corner, she saw Sean searching the linen closet frantically.

He didn't notice her presence and continued searching. She gaped, unable to form words as he threw towels and sheets onto the floor around him. What was he doing? It was beyond the pale. She was just about to shout his name when he spun about and turned his attention to her small bedside table. The flat was one long, thin room, with her bed taking up the space beside the linen closet. It was then that she noticed he'd pulled her bed apart and shifted the mattress.

"Sean! What are you doing?" she cried, throwing her hands into the air.

He faced her with a start, cheeks red. "Nothing. I'm looking for something."

"You're making a huge mess. Even more so than usual. And you're violating my privacy. It's not appropriate to poke through someone's drawers and cupboards without asking. You know that, right?"

"What does it matter?" His eyes narrowed. "Are you hiding something from me, little sister?"

Her eyes widened. "What? No, of course I'm not. What would I be hiding?"

"You know what I'm talking about." He lurched towards her, a menacing look on his face.

Charmaine startled at the sudden change in his demeanour. She shrank away from him. "I have no idea what you mean."

"Where's the jewellery, Chaz?"

"Jewellery?"

"Mum talked to you about everything. She would've told you about the jewellery. I overheard her on the phone. She said she'd put it in a safe place, but when I went back to Newcastle, you'd rented out her house and I couldn't find it anywhere."

"You went into the house? You can't do that, Sean. We don't live there anymore."

"Where's all Mum's stuff?" His voice rose to a shout, and he grabbed her arms, squeezing them.

"Ouch, that hurts. I got rid of most of it. I kept a few things, like a diary and some knickknacks that were meaningful to me. I didn't think you'd want anything."

He spun on his heel and stalked to the other side of the flat and back again, grey eyes flashing. He knocked a vase of wildflowers from the coffee table, sending it smashing to the floor. "Don't lie to me. Where are Mum's things?"

He grabbed her again, this time a look of desperation painting his face red.

"Sean, what's wrong? Why are you acting like this? You're scaring me." She tried to shrug him off, but he wouldn't release her.

Then he threw his hands to his sides in frustration. "You won't understand. I need money, Chaz. I've borrowed from some dangerous people, and they're after me. If you don't give me Mum's jewellery, I don't know what will happen to me."

"Why did you borrow money?"

"I like sports. Okay?" He ran his fingers through his hair, then slumped onto the couch.

"Okay . . .?" Where was this going? She'd only ever seen her brother show a passing interest in sports. And what did that have to do with money? Realisation dawned. "You're gambling? On sports? You know that's a good way to lose money, right? Mum always told us that. No one wins a bet but a bookie. Remember?"

He laughed. "I remember, but then I thought about how good I was with numbers. I figured out this system and how to make it work at the local casino. And I was getting good at it, too, but they kicked me out. So, I moved on to the TAB. And I won. I won enough money to live on for months. I quit my job and bought a motorbike. I thought it was the beginning of something amazing."

Charmaine sat gingerly beside him. "But then you lost. Right?"

He nodded. "I came home to see Mum before she died, and she lent me some money. I didn't tell her what it was for, just that I needed it. It was part of our inheritance and I lost it."

Charmaine's head spun. She couldn't believe what she was hearing. "You went to your sick mother and asked her to fund your gambling debts with her hard-earned money? How could you do that?"

"Don't pretend to be a saint, Chaz," he snarled. "It doesn't suit you."

She leapt to her feet, hands pressed to her forehead in disbelief. "I'm not saying that I'm a saint, but I certainly wouldn't burden my dying mother with my gambling debt. That's cruel, Sean. And you lied to me. You took our inheritance, and you used it without asking me. That was mine as much as it was yours."

"Get over yourself, Chaz. You were always the favourite. Mum took care of everything for you. I needed the help—you didn't. I'm always the one who ends up in trouble. No one cares about what happens to me. I have to figure it out on my own."

His words made no sense. His face was bathed in sweat, and his eyes darted in every direction. She didn't recognise the person he'd become. Tears pooled in her eyes but she blinked them away.

"You have to leave," Charmaine said, pointing to the door. "I can't have you stay here. You need help—you need to be arrested. I always suspected you'd taken the money, but I let you convince me I was wrong, that I was crazy to think something like that about my own brother. But now the truth comes out — I was right."

"I'm not leaving," he said.

"Leave, or I'm calling the police."

At first she thought he would hit her, but then he gathered his things into a duffel bag. He stopped in front of her, eyes wild. "I'm going to find that jewellery."

She threw her hands up in the air. "I don't have the jewellery, Sean. I don't have anything at all, thanks to you." Her heart pounded in her ears, panic worming its way up her spine.

He stormed from the flat, slamming the door so hard that the walls shook. Charmaine stood in the centre of the room, shaking, her fingers pressed to her lips. She'd seen that side of her brother in the past, but not for a long time. She should've listened to her instincts about him. She always fell for his charm—even as a young girl, she could never stay mad at him. But this was the last time. She wouldn't let it happen again.

Watson emerged from wherever he'd been hiding and wrapped his tail around her legs in silence. She bent to pick him up, held him against her cheek and stroked his back.

"What am I going to do, Watson?"

* * *

The first thing she did was call the locksmith to have the locks changed on her flat. Next she opened her set of forty-eight watercolour crayons. She'd saved up for them when she started working at a restaurant in Brisbane a year earlier. She'd looked at them in the shop window for weeks before finally taking the plunge. They were perfect — the colours, the texture, the quality. Everything she drew with them felt like a masterpiece compared to the chunky, cheap crayons she'd used in the past. These were divine. She treasured them and used them daily.

She opened the back of the case and pulled out a long necklace covered in diamonds, then a matching tennis bracelet. She studied each piece, fingered the diamonds, then shoved them into her purse.

With a sigh, she reached for a hat, then donned a pair of oversized sunglasses. With one last look around the flat, she slipped out into the twilight and down the back staircase. Watson came with her, but stopped at the bottom of the steps to watch her head into town.

The bank would only be open for another thirty minutes. She'd have to hurry. She glanced back down the street and up in the other direction, careful she wasn't being followed. Her pulse thundered in her ears, drowning out the sound of passersby who were laughing and chatting as everyone headed for home or out to eat together. Some recognised her and waved hello. She waved back, but kept moving. She didn't have time for distractions.

Inside the bank, it didn't take long to get a safe deposit box set up. She signed the forms and soon found herself alone with the box and a key. She put the jewellery into the box and shut the lid, then locked it and called the staff member into the room to put the box away. Then she tucked the key into her bra and walked out the door.

"Chaz!" A man's voice sent her heart into her throat.

Bradford jogged across the street, and she inhaled a long, calming breath at the sight of him as her pulse slowed to a normal rate. "Hi."

"Hi," he said, offering her a shy grin. It looked good on him. "I haven't seen you since our coffee date. I've been meaning to call. I got a new phone."

She shook her head. "Glad to hear it."

"I'd love to go out somewhere together. If you're still available." He questioned.

"That sounds great."

"*Surf and Sea* on Saturday night? I'll pick you up at seven."

As she watched him walk away, her thoughts returned to the events of the evening. The locksmith would be there in the morning, but in the meantime, she had to spend the night alone in that flat with Sean wandering the streets. As far as she knew, he hadn't copied her keys, but she'd let him take them often enough that he might've. Besides, the door to her flat wasn't exactly sturdy or criminal proof. And she now knew for certain that her brother was a criminal.

Where had he gone? Would he be back? He'd promised he would find the jewellery, and she believed him. But it should be safe in the bank vault for now.

Maybe he'd decide that a dead sister was better than a live one and as her only living relative he would inherit her estate. She should make a will, leaving her estate to someone other than her brother. She'd go home and look online for a simple will kit. Not that she had much to leave behind, but she did have something. Something he clearly wanted. Whether or not he'd kill for it, she couldn't say, but she didn't want to wait around to find out.

She looked both ways before crossing the road, then hurried back to her flat. Inside, she pressed a chair up against the doorknob after locking it. Then she sat on the couch, eating macaroni and cheese and watching comedy reruns with Watson curled up beside her. The one good thing that'd come of it all was that she had her flat to herself again. And it felt good.

Ten

EVIE SET a dozen fresh peaches in her basket and then reached for a bag of cherries. Summer fruit was her favourite. She loved the cherries best of all. Throughout the year, she couldn't wait for summer to arrive so she could eat fruit all day long. She never tired of it. However, she should've thought through her choice of basket a little better when she stepped into the grocery shop. A trolley would've been preferable to a basket on her arm — now it was so full and heavy, it was leaving a large red welt on her forearm.

She shifted the basket and headed for the egg aisle. When she saw David looking through the cartons of free-range eggs, she almost spun around to head in the other direction, but he noticed her before she could manage it.

With a smile planted on her face, she told him good morning, then wandered over to stand beside him, looking for her preferred eggs.

"It's nice to see you again," David said.

She nodded. "And you. How are you settling into life on the island?"

"It's going well. The kids have been very welcoming —

their parents, too. Plus, I've taken up snorkelling. I've never seen such a variety of coloured fish and coral before in my life. It's stunning."

"Snorkelling is one of my favourite things to do. Everyone on the island does it," Evie replied. "It's so relaxing. It doesn't matter how stressful my day has been—if I can get some time in the water, looking at the fish and the reef, all that anxiety simply lifts from my shoulders."

"I know exactly what you mean," he said, studying her with a grin. "I wanted to talk to you about something. It's kind of awkward, so I'm not sure how to broach the subject."

"Oh?" Her cheeks warmed, and she wished she could be anywhere else. She could see where he was taking the conversation, and it made her uncomfortable.

"I ran into your sister the other day outside the bookshop."

"Did you?"

"Yes. I didn't realise you had a twin."

"I must not have mentioned it," she said, reaching for a carton of eggs and placing it on top of her peaches. The basket was unbearably heavy now.

"It's disconcerting how much alike you look."

"I know—it's strange for me as well. I don't see her often, so when she visits, I have to look at myself in the mirror each morning and remind myself we're two different people."

"Really? You do?" His brow furrowed.

She laughed. "No, I'm kidding."

"Oh, of course. Anyway, I asked her out on a date, and we're going to dinner together soon. I can't do it this week—I had to postpone—but we'll catch up next week. I hope you don't mind."

She inhaled a quick breath. "No, of course I don't mind."

"Great. I'm glad to hear it. That's a relief. I don't want to step on any toes, and I know sometimes relationships between siblings can be complicated."

"Not at all. I hope you have a lovely time together." She should tell him, should spit it out. *Emily is married!* She should shout it, stamp her feet, do something to let him know. But of course, if she did that, he'd think she was simply being spiteful, hateful or petty. Emily would explain the situation in a way that made Evie the villain, as she always did. And Evie and David would have to avoid each other for the rest of his time on the island.

Evie was exhausted by all the drama Emily put her through. She'd had enough of it. If Emily wanted to squander her own marriage by dating someone else, that was her business. Evie wasn't about to get involved. Not again.

* * *

After a full day of packing books into boxes and wiping down bookshelves to get rid of the dust, along with taking a thorough inventory, Evie was exhausted. Her back ached, her throat was raw, and a headache had begun pounding against her temples about two hours earlier.

Emily had gone home at lunchtime complaining about being used as slave labour, and Evie hadn't seen or heard from her since. Janice had stayed until five and had kept up a steady stream of upbeat conversation for the entire day. She was truly a life saver, and Evie had never felt so old in all her life. Every single part of her body ached, and all she wanted to do was collapse in her bed and go to sleep. But she had to eat first or she'd keel over.

She nudged the last box into the back storage room with her knees, not attempting to lift it on her own. She removed her dust mask and reached for her purse where it hung on the coatrack by the kitchen. When she stepped outside, the moon was already creeping up the dark edge of the sky. A few stars sparkled overhead, and the hum and shush of the ocean sighing against the dock nearby gave her an immediate sense of peace and wellbeing. It was all going to be okay.

The amount of work involved in renovating the bookshop was overwhelming to her at times. It was why she'd avoided doing it for so long. But now that she'd been forced to take the step, she was glad. It was well past due, and she was excited to see what the space would look like when the work was complete.

"Evie, wait for me," Penny called out to her from behind.

Evie stopped and turned to see her friend speed walking from the direction of the primary school. She folded her arms. "What are you doing at the school?"

Penny laughed. "I wasn't at the school. I went for a walk. What are you doing?"

"I was going to eat at the Thai restaurant down by Betsy's shop. I'm starved."

"I'm hungry too. Would you like some company?"

"That would be great, if you don't mind eating with someone covered in dust and no doubt smelling as though I haven't showered in a week."

"You look and smell fine." Penny looped a hand through Evie's arm. "It's so nice to see you."

They walked arm in arm together to the restaurant and asked to sit outside. They were seated at a small round table beneath an awning, with a tealight candle flickering between them. They each ordered a meal and a glass of wine. A gentle breeze lifted Evie's hair from her neck, cutting through the humidity.

She sighed as she leaned back in her chair. "It feels good to get off my feet."

"How's the renovation coming?" Penny sipped from her glass of water.

"It's slow and I'm wrecked. But I think it'll be good when it's finished."

"I'm sure it'll be great."

"The main problem, of course, is that it won't be finished for months."

"Oh, no!" Penny's eyes widened. "Really? Can you manage for that long without an income?"

"I'll scrape by. I've put aside a little nest egg. It's not a lot, but it was meant to be for my retirement. I don't want to use that to live on. I'm going to die homeless if I'm not careful." Her hollow laugh and attempt to make light of the situation only made her sound more pathetic to her own ears.

Penny rested a hand on her arm. "I'm sorry, sweetie. I know what you mean. I've done something similar — I'm grateful my parents gave me the beach house, or I don't know what I'd have done."

Their food arrived—a steaming-hot beef massaman with meat so tender, it fell apart when Evie stuck her fork in it, and a plate of Pad Thai noodles dotted with peanuts and pieces of chicken. Evie spooned coconut rice into her bowl and then a serving from each of the dishes. Her mouth watered at the sight and scent of the food.

"How's your sister?" Penny asked around a mouthful of rice and curry.

"She's good. I still don't know what's happened, but I think it's something to do with her marriage. She was staying with Mum and Dad for a while, and they seemed to think she needed a break from her life. But I wonder if it's something more serious than that because she's been staying with me for a couple of weeks now and she hasn't mentioned anything about returning home."

"Maybe they're struggling," Penny offered.

Evie shrugged. "It seems likely. I'm not surprised—my

sister can be difficult to live with. I should know. We lived together for years."

"Marriage is hard," Penny said, her voice soft.

Evie set down her fork. "Are you okay, honey?"

Penny's eyes filled with tears. "Not really."

"What's wrong?"

"Rowan isn't happy. I was worried this might happen, and now that it is, I don't know what to do about it. He left his high-powered career as a journalist to work with me in the office at the animal refuge. And now he's dissatisfied."

"Has he told you that?"

"No, not in as many words. He pretends that he's fine, but he's not. He's grumpy and irritable. He shouts at the staff and stares into the distance. He doesn't have any patience with me. I don't know what to do. We're at each other's throats all the time. And we haven't celebrated our first anniversary yet. What if my marriage is over before we pass the year mark?" Penny pressed both hands to her face, covering her eyes.

Evie patted her shoulder. "It's going to be all right. I know it will. The two of you love each other so much. You can't give up."

"I'm not giving up," Penny sobbed. "But I don't know what to do. We got that big government grant, so we have more responsibilities than ever. I'm working all the time, but I can't take time off. He says he's bored and lonely. He's probably feeling the stress of everything that's happened with Buck going to prison and then being let out on parole, although that's another thing he refuses to talk about." She sighed and reached for a napkin to blow her nose.

"Has he thought about going to see a doctor? Maybe he's depressed."

"Ha!" Penny spat. "See a doctor? I can't get him to take a multivitamin. When I suggest the doctor's office, he laughs and walks away."

Evie's eyes widened. "That doesn't sound like Rowan at all."

"I know. He's not himself."

"The arrest and parole have effected all of us more than we realise, I'm sure of it." Evie gulped a mouthful of wine. "I'm on edge all the time. Bea has lost weight from being so worried she'll run into Buck in the street or that he'll come looking for her because of the evidence she found against him in the cave."

"I saw him," Penny said.

Evie gaped. "What? When?"

"I was walking to Bea's, and he was headed in the opposite direction. I stopped and spoke with him. He was nice, quiet. I was upset and probably yelled at him—I can't remember what I said. But he looked sad. I felt horrible about it. He says he's innocent."

"Do you believe him?"

"I don't know," Penny replied. "I don't know what to think about any of this. I thought Rowan and I would be happy together. That we didn't need fancy careers if we had each other. And I thought that when I found my biological father, he'd be a nice man with a good job who would take me out to dinner or to see a show — not some psychopath who killed my grandmother."

"What does your mum say about it all?"

Penny laughed. "She won't talk about it. I'm surrounded by people who won't talk about their problems. It's frustrating."

"She probably blames herself, you know." Evie shook her head as she imagined what Penny's mother must be going through. How hard it must've been for her when she discovered her own mother's dead body and the police questioned her lover over the murder.

"I'm sure you're right." Penny played with her fork, turning the rice over and over in her bowl. "She's had a hard life. I can't blame her for not wanting to think about the worst thing that ever happened to her."

"Especially since there was never any closure. She was so young, and the police investigated the case for years and came up empty. No one has ever paid for what happened. She had to get on with her life and put it behind her, so she did. We can't blame her for that."

"You're right. I've been too hard on her." Penny wiped her nose with the napkin again. "I'm a terrible daughter."

"No, you're not."

"And a bad wife."

Evie sighed and squeezed Penny's arm. "No, you're not. You're a good wife, daughter and friend. We all have our hard days."

"Maybe we got married too quickly. I knew we shouldn't have rushed in, but we've known each other so long..."

"You didn't get married too quickly," Evie said, although she'd wondered about that herself when Penny had announced their engagement.

"We were virtually enemies up until last year. And we got married so fast. We're still getting to know one another as life partners and friends. I used to think I hated him and now I love him so much, but it's hard."

"From what I've heard, marriage can be difficult. I don't have firsthand experience of it and my parents have always been blissfully happy, but I know my sister's relationship is often up and down."

"What should I do?" Penny asked, eyes glimmering.

"I think you need to communicate with him about it," Evie said.

"What if he still won't talk?"

"*Make* him talk. The two of you are partners now—you have to discuss things. Communication is so important in a relationship."

"I know you're right."

"I had a serious boyfriend once. If we'd communicated more, perhaps things would've turned out differently. I often wonder about it."

"I remember you mentioning a boyfriend, but you've never told me anything about him."

"We lived together for almost a decade," Evie replied. "I thought we would spend the rest of our lives together. But we didn't talk enough, so I didn't know he was unhappy — I thought we were both settled and strong in our love for one another. But I was wrong."

"What happened?"

"He left me for someone else out of the blue."

"I'm so sorry, honey. Do you think Rowan's going to do that?" Penny's asked, her brow furrowed.

Evie shook her head. "No, I don't. But my point is, you need to communicate. My boyfriend and I didn't talk about our relationship enough. I didn't know he was unhappy—I didn't see the signs. He didn't like to talk, and I didn't make him. Then he was gone before I realised what had happened."

"That must've been hard."

"It was devastating. It changed the entire course of my life. I had so many plans and an entire life built around him — a future marriage and children, an expanding photography business, a lovely group of friends. I lost it all that day. When he told me our relationship was over, that he'd met someone else, I left town. I moved back to Coral Island and started this bookshop."

"You haven't ever told me that story," Penny said. "Thank you for sharing it with me. I'm sorry you went through that."

"Thanks, but it's all part of what makes me who I am. I'm not upset about it anymore, or at least, I'm not most of the time. Every now and then, I get a pang of regret."

"What might've been," Penny mused.

"Exactly. So, don't make the same mistake—talk to Rowan before things get any worse. If you want your marriage to work, both of you have to sacrifice and do whatever it takes. And you have to communicate."

"You're absolutely right, of course." Penny studied the food in her bowl. "I'm going to talk to him tomorrow."

"I'm sure you'll work things out. As I said before, you love each other. And love can overcome a lot."

"But you loved each other, didn't you?"

"I thought we did. But I suppose I was wrong."

Penny sighed. "Let's change the subject. I don't want to talk about my failing marriage anymore or I'll start bawling at this table. What's next for your renovation?" She scooped up some curry and ate it.

"I have to get some new bookshelves and couches. I'm going to catch the ferry to Airlie Beach tomorrow to put in an order. Do you want to come with me?"

"Yes, please! Picking out furniture is exactly what I need to lift my mood."

Eleven

"I CAN'T BELIEVE you convinced me to go bushwalking with you," Bradford said as he stepped over a cow pat in the field below Elias's house.

Charmaine threw her head back and laughed. "You must know this area like the back of your hand. You grew up here."

He smirked. "I know it too well. I wanted to take you somewhere luxurious and spoil you. Instead, I'm sweating through my shirt and jeans, and sliding around in cow poop in my Italian loafers."

"I told you to dress comfortably."

"I'm not sure I like this whole idea of us taking turns on deciding what to do on a date." He reached for her hand and held it gently as they walked. Their joined hands swung in time with their footsteps.

"You took me to a fancy restaurant for our first date, and now I'm taking you on one of my favourite walks for our second. It's going well, by the way."

She couldn't believe how confident she felt. Ever since they'd had dinner at the *Surf and Sea* restaurant the previous Friday night, she'd been a different person. Conversation with him came so easily that her anxiety simply vanished. He was fun, lighthearted and warm. She'd been so intimidated by his handsome, athletic looks at first, but now she was completely at ease in his presence. Banter didn't exactly come naturally to her, but she'd found herself exchanging witty small talk with him and she wasn't awkward about it.

"I'm glad it's going well," he said. "By the way, where are we going?"

"The cliffs over here are amazing. They have a spectacular view over the open ocean, and the cliff faces themselves are so black and jagged. I love to sit at the top and mull."

"That sounds dangerous."

"I don't sit too close to the edge—unless I'm feeling adventurous, of course."

He shook his head. "I had no idea you were such a daredevil."

"There's more to me than meets the eye."

He winked at her. "Clearly. Okay, the cliffs. Then we head into town and I buy you a nice coffee at Bea's."

"That sounds perfect," she said.

"How are things at work?"

"Pretty good. I sold my first painting today."

"Really? That's fantastic. You're a professional artist now. There's no turning back."

She blushed at his words. "I don't know about that, but it's definitely a boost. Betsy has hardly been at work lately, so I'm basically doing everything the way I want. She's so distracted by this whole thing with Buck and taking care of Samantha. Her focus is on her family, and I can respect that. It's why she hired me — to give her some flexibility in her schedule. And this way, I can try out new ideas, something she's encouraged me to do."

"What kind of ideas?"

"I've moved the ordering system online. Betsy wrote orders into her ledger by hand, and she also counted stock and planned trips to the flower market that way. I've put all of it into a web-based system we can access from our mobile phones. Now I don't have to lug that big ledger with me everywhere, I can see what stock I have in the shop at a glance wherever I am, and I can place orders while I'm watching my favourite TV show."

"Good for you. I hope Betsy can keep up."

"She'll love it once she gets the hang of it. It's so easy to use."

"I wish I had someone like you working for my business. It's so hard to find anyone with a bit of self-motivation." He ran his fingers through his hair, setting it on end. "But I suppose you wouldn't want to trade in flowers for yachts."

She laughed. "Not at the moment. I'm enjoying my work, and it puts me in contact with brides who need wedding planners. Between the two jobs, I'm finally putting a little bit of money into my savings account each month. I've never been able to do that before. I've always thought I'd live my life in quiet desperation, but I'm happy. You know, apart from the whole psycho-brother thing."

"Still having issues there?" He frowned.

She shrugged. "I'll tell you all about it over coffee. Let's climb this hill. It's going to take all our breath for a while."

She tugged him by the hand, and they set out to ascend the hill that led up to the cliffs. The trail they were taking was a cow track in a field adjacent to Bradford's childhood house. Below them, the road wound down to a private cove where Bea's beach cottage stood.

Bea had moved in with Aidan, so she wasn't likely to be home. But perhaps they should drop by anyway. Charmaine hadn't seen the beach cottage—she'd only heard about it. And she liked the idea of stopping by with Bea's brother to take a look. Maybe she could offer to rent the place from Bea now that it was empty.

"Is your sister renting out the cottage?" she asked.

"Yes. She said she was going to clean it up and get it ready for a tenant. I think she's there today."

"Do you think I should rent it?"

"Yeah, why not? It's a cute place. Bea and Dani did a good job fixing it up."

"Is it too isolated?"

"Well, no one lives close by. Dad's house is up the hill, but there's no line of sight between the two places. Of course, Bea lived at the cottage on her own for months and she loved it. So, I guess it depends if you like isolation and privacy or not."

"I do." She was puffing now. The exertion was invigorating. She loved to get out in nature and enjoyed exercising outdoors. It was one of her favourite parts of living on Coral Island. How easy it was to get out and about and explore the natural beauty of the place.

"Let's stop under this tree for a minute," she said. "The sun is hot today. I wish I'd worn a hat."

"Take your time," Bradford said. "There's no rush."

While they rested, Charmaine tented a hand over her eyes to scan the clifftops. It wasn't far now—maybe a few hundred metres more to go. Then they could head back and slurp down a delicious iced coffee. All the extra calories wouldn't matter after a walk like that.

A flash of red on the cliffs caught her eye. What was it? A person, definitely a person. She squinted and pointed. "Someone's walking up ahead. Do you think it's your dad?"

The person walked towards the edge of the cliff.

"Too short. And he doesn't wear red."

"Is that Betsy?" Just as she asked the question, the figure disappeared beyond the cliff face. "And did she just leap off the cliff or decide to traverse the rocky cliff face?"

Bradford frowned. "It didn't look like a leap, but Betsy has to be in her eighties. Why is she tackling a cliff?"

"No idea. She's such an odd duck sometimes. I don't know why she does half the things I catch her doing."

"Like what?"

"The other day, I came into the room, and she was shredding all those old photos—the ones of her with famous people that she had hanging up in the shop. I was so shocked, I didn't say anything. I hope they were copies. She didn't look at me. She just kept on shredding. It was so strange."

"That is odd."

"You know, your sister and her friends have a theory about Betsy."

"Do they?" He fixed his gaze on Charmaine. "What's the theory?"

"That she's a fugitive on the run."

He huffed. "What? Betsy? Hardly."

"I don't know—maybe they're right. How well do we know the people we see every day? I mean, to me, she's this lovely old lady who gave me a job and a place to live, and who brings me a coffee and a muffin for breakfast when I open up the shop. She's thoughtful and kind. She takes care of her granddaughter and runs a reasonably successful boutique florist shop. But she could also be an international criminal on the run from the FBI. Right?" Even as she said the words, they sounded so ludicrous that she had to laugh.

Bradford guffawed. "Beatrice gets a little dramatic sometimes. There's no way Betsy Norton is a criminal."

"Although, her brother *is* out on parole—maybe it runs in the family." There was that. It seemed impossible that Betsy could be related to a murderer. She was the nicest little old lady in the world, but she was his alibi and had paid for him to get out of prison on bail. Two complicating factors in the equation.

"I suppose that's true. But the real question right now is, where is she?"

They waited another half an hour in the shade before Betsy's red silk kaftan appeared at the top of the cliff. She leaned on a walking stick, and each step was slow and steady. Then she crested the cliff and headed down the field in their direction.

"Hide," Charmaine whispered, ducking behind the tree. When Betsy passed them, they watched her back retreat towards a car parked in the field.

"Why didn't we notice that car was there before?" Bradford asked, his brow furrowed.

"I have no idea. It's so strange — does she take dangerous walks along cliff faces regularly? You think you know a person..."

"I'm calling Bea." Bradford dialled before Charmaine could object and held his mobile phone to his ear. He described what they'd seen to Bea, then hung up the phone.

"What did she say?" Charmaine asked, still whispering.

"Betsy's gone. You don't have to whisper," he replied with a laugh. "And she said she's coming."

"Coming here?"

"Yep. She was working at the cottage, like I thought. She'll be here in five minutes."

"She didn't have to do that. I'm sure it's nothing."

"Bea loves nothing more than a good mystery. I couldn't stop her from coming now if I tried."

When Beatrice joined them, she was barely puffing. She looked fit and tanned, and wore a hat. Her arms gleamed with freshly applied suncream.

"You came prepared," Bradford quipped as he kissed her cheek.

"I can't believe you two are out here walking in the heat of the day without hats," she admonished them. "You're both adults, you know."

Charmaine stifled a smile. "Yes, Bea. You're right, of course. So, what do you think about Betsy? Why would she go for a walk over that cliff?" She pointed in the direction Betsy had gone.

Bea pressed her hands to her hips. "Let's go and see."

The three of them traipsed up the hill. When they stood at the top, overlooking the cliff face and the ocean, Charmaine let her hands drop loose at her sides and inhaled a long, deep breath of fresh, salty air. The wind was strong, buffeting each of them and lifting Charmaine's hair from the back of her neck, cooling the sweat that coated her skin.

"Where did she go from here?" Bea asked, scanning the cliffs.

"Over there, I think," Bradford replied. He grinned. "This is silly. Why are we tracing Betsy's steps? She went for a walk. You know how much she loves fishing. She was probably scoping out a good spot."

"Is this a good fishing spot?" Charmaine asked.

He shrugged. "It's dangerous. You'd have to stand out there on those rocks." He waved an arm towards the base of the cliffs. Charmaine shivered.

"Do you remember that cave where I found the evidence against her brother, Buck?" Bea's voice was loud with excitement.

"Yes," Charmaine replied.

"It's just over there. Maybe she was visiting the cave. Maybe she was the shadowy figure I saw the last time I was here, the one who led me to the cave in the first place. Given the size, it could've been her."

Bradford followed Bea and Charmaine down the narrow, winding trail that ran through the rocks and along the cliff face to the opening. It wasn't far to the mouth of the cave.

They stopped outside and looked it over before climbing inside.

The opening was short, but wide. Bradford had to duck his head to get inside. "Why would Betsy come down here? Didn't you already take the box to the police? There wasn't anything else left behind, was there?"

Bea stopped and surveyed the darkened cave. The floor was sand, and there was a narrow trickle of water running through the centre of it to a pool in the back where the roof sloped down to meet the sand. "I don't know. I should've looked around more, I suppose. But I was so excited to find the box, I didn't think to look for anything else."

Charmaine stepped around the cave cautiously, careful not to get her brand-new joggers wet. "Where was the box?"

Bea tapped the sand with one foot. "Right here."

Charmaine took her time wandering around the edges of the cave. She found a place where the sand had been dug up recently. There were small footprints all around it, and the sand was disturbed in an oval shape. "Look at this."

"I bet she dug something up," Bradford said when he reached Charmaine. He squatted, reached out a hand, and began shovelling the loose sand aside. It was damp, but easy to move since it'd already been loosened. After a while, he stopped. "Nothing there."

"Whatever it was is gone," Bea said.

They searched the cave for a while longer and were about to leave when Charmaine squealed in surprise and bent at the waist to look more closely. She was beside the rear wall of the cave, and something had sparkled when she moved. She reached for it and picked it up. It was nestled in the palm of her hand when Bradford and Bea arrived on either side of her.

"What is it?"

"I think it's a diamond," Charmaine whispered, eyes wide.

"Wow, you're right—it looks like a diamond. I wonder

what it's doing in here." Bradford touched it with a fingertip. "You should keep it."

"Or report it to the police," Bea added.

"I suppose someone might've lost it." Bradford scratched his chin. "But if they don't claim it after a month or so, I think you get to keep it."

"I'm not going to get excited yet. I'll give it to the police, and I'm sure they'll test it to see if it's a diamond. If it is, it's a big one."

"Very big," Bea agreed. "Several carats, I'd say."

They headed back outside. Charmaine blinked in the glare of sunshine. She held the diamond closer to her face. It was dull, not as shiny as she'd thought it would be — it looked old. Now that she could see it more clearly, it was shaped as though it'd been set in a necklace or ring once upon a time.

They climbed the track again and headed for Bea's cottage. She poured water into three glasses.

"I'm sorry I can't offer you more than this. Everything is over at Aidan's now, although I'm leaving these glasses, kitchenware and some of the furniture behind. Since we don't need it and I bought it to match the cottage.'"

Then the three of them sat on the porch overlooking her quaint little beach.

"This is beautiful," Charmaine said. "I can see why you like it here."

"Thank you. I hate to give it up to a renter," Bea replied.

Bradford shot Charmaine an encouraging look. She drew a deep breath. "I'm interested, if you're willing to consider me."

"Really? I would love that. It would be a huge relief to have someone I know living here rather than a perfect stranger."

"I'm not sure if I can afford it, but if I can, this place would be perfect for me."

"We can work something out," Bea replied. "I don't want

it sitting empty. That's the main thing. Someone should enjoy it, and I'd hate to see it fall into ruin after all the work I put into it. But what about your flat? Will Betsy mind?"

"I don't think it will matter to her. Yes, I'll miss the flat and the free rent, but it's probably time for me to get something a little bigger. A place of my own. I can't rely on Betsy's goodwill forever. And I need a little more space and a place outside to sit and think. I love being out here on the porch. I can't do that at my flat. I have to look out the window instead."

If she had a new place to live, perhaps she could finally start the life she'd always dreamed of having. She was happier than she'd been in years. Bradford sat beside her, and a thrill of anticipation over the future ran through her body as she looked at him. He was warm and kind, positive and gentle. The kind of man she needed in her life. She didn't know how things would proceed between the two of them, but no matter what happened, she was stronger, more grounded and more capable than she'd ever been.

All she wanted was to put down roots on Coral Island and stay for a long time. If only her brother would leave. His presence on the island kept her uneasy, even though she hadn't seen him again since she kicked him out of her flat. Perhaps he'd moved on, but it wasn't likely, given his threat. There must be a way to get him to leave. But she'd always wonder if he would return, and the thought of that made her stomach churn.

Twelve

EVIE POURED orange juice into the punch bowl. Nerves flittered up her spine. Book club was that night, but she had no idea how any of it would work. The new bookshelves she and Charmaine picked out in Airlie Beach had arrived that morning and were pushed up against the walls. The floor had been temporarily fixed with sheets of plywood and was a complete hodgepodge of mismatched materials. She'd pulled chairs into a circle next to a table piled with finger foods, and only hoped not many people would show.

Beatrice poked her head through the front door. "Hello?"

Evie waved.

"Is book club still on? I wasn't sure, with all the construction and everything."

"Still on," Evie replied. "Come in. You're a little early— that's all. I'm sure the others will be arriving soon."

"Wow," Bea said, scanning the room. "We've had the partition up between the café and your shop, so I haven't seen inside lately. You've done a lot — I love these new bookshelves."

"Thanks. I probably shouldn't have spent so much money, but I figure they'll last forever."

"Absolutely! They'll be worth every penny."

Just then, the lights went out and the entire bookshop was thrown into darkness. A crack of thunder in the distance made Evie jump. "Oh, no. Everyone will be here soon. I hope the lights come back on quickly or it's going to be a little awkward bumping into each other in the dark."

"I'll get some candles from the café," Bea said.

"Thanks, but I have plenty in the storeroom."

The two of them found the candles and lighters and went about the bookshop setting candles in strategic locations. Before long, the entire room looked like a romantic setting from a movie. People began to arrive and find their places. Everyone exclaimed over the pretty candlelight, and Evie had to admit that the multicoloured floor and the half-painted walls looked much more appealing in the flickering golden light.

David came in last with Emily on his arm and waved to Evie. By that time, she was fully occupied getting drinks for people and answering questions about the renovation. She waved back and watched as he and Emily found seats. Emily came to the table to get drinks for them both.

"Loving the atmosphere," she said. "Very romantic."

"Thanks. The power went out. I think there's a storm coming."

"Sorry I couldn't help set up. My headache isn't so bad now."

"I'm glad you're feeling better. I don't mind setting up by myself—I didn't have to do too much. I decided on finger food straight from the freezer section."

Emily laughed. "Good choice."

It warmed her heart to see her sister happy and for the two of them to have a conversation that didn't involve yelling.

They got on well some of the time, but Emily's jealousy got in the way the rest of the time. Jealousy was no way to live, Evie had decided many years earlier. The two of them had always been highly competitive — competing for attention, awards, friendships and boys. But Evie had decided to give up competing when it finally caused her so much heartbreak that she lost the will to fight. She only hoped Emily would share her desire for reconciliation so the two of them could be sisters again.

The group was halfway through their discussion questions for the current month's book when the door swung open and a man stepped through the doorway. Charmaine gasped and rushed to greet him. They spoke together in hushed tones while the discussion continued. Evie watched them, half distracted, wondering who the man was and why Charmaine had such red cheeks. She got up from her chair and quietly made her way to the front door.

"Hi, I'm Evie," she whispered, stretching out her hand towards him.

He glared at her, then shook it. "Sean. Pleased to meet you."

Evie glanced at Charmaine, who looked distressed. "This is my brother."

"Oh, yes. Of course. How nice to see you at book club. Will you join us?"

"Book club? No, thank you. I have somewhere else I have to be just as soon as my little sister does what I've asked her to do."

Evie looked back and forth between the two of them. Charmaine stayed silent, her lips pressed together until they were like a thin, pale line.

"Go away, Sean. I'll talk to you about it later. I'm busy now."

He grunted. "I don't care if you're busy. I need it now, and

I can't wait any longer. I think I've been more than patient with you."

"I'm sorry," Evie interrupted, provoking Sean's face to become thunderous. "What are we talking about?"

"Nothing," Charmaine quickly responded. "Sean, I can't help you now. There's a roomful of people here, and you're being rude."

"Then come with me," he said, grabbing her upper arm between his fingers and making Charmaine cry out in pain.

Bradford rose from his seat and strode across the circle. The conversation drifted into silence as everyone turned to watch.

"Everything okay here?"

"It's fine," Sean snapped.

Evie's heart raced. The last thing she wanted to do was cause conflict tonight, of all nights. But if she didn't get Charmaine's brother to leave, things were about to become heated. She could tell by the looks on the faces of both Sean and Bradford.

"Sean was just leaving," Charmaine said, wrenching her arm free of his grasp.

Sean's expression turned jovial. He raised both hands in surrender. "I'm leaving. I don't know why you're making such a fuss about nothing, little sister."

He reached out, and before Evie could protest, he grabbed one of the candlesticks by the doorway and slipped outside. She gaped after him — what could he want with a half-used candle? Maybe it was his way of showing off his rebellion. But whatever it was, she was relieved he'd left. Perhaps now they could get back to discussing the book.

When she faced the group, they all quickly looked away and began whispering among themselves. Her cheeks must be bright red, but there wasn't anything she could do about what'd happened. She didn't know why Charmaine's brother was there. And now she understood why Charmaine had been so reluctant to see him all that time. He was obviously the type of person accustomed to getting his way, and he seemed a little off-kilter. The way he'd grabbed Charmaine's arm was disturbing.

"Are you all right, Chaz?" She slipped an arm around Charmaine's waist and walked with her back to her seat.

"I'm fine. A little rattled—that's all."

"Do you want to talk about it?"

"Not now," Charmaine replied as she sat down. Bradford sat with her, his countenance dark.

"Okay, well, whenever you're ready to talk, I'm ready to listen."

"Thanks, Evie."

Evie returned to her place and resumed overseeing the book club discussion, but her thoughts remained on the front door and an uneasy feeling that Sean wasn't finished disrupting their event.

"Who thinks the protagonist could have grown a little faster?" she asked.

The group laughed, and several readers nodded.

"He was a slug," Bea said with a shake of her head.

"Sloths learn faster," Charmaine agreed. Her cheeks were still red. Evie was glad to see her joining in. She usually sat in silence, listening to the interactions. She tapped her pen lid against the notepad in her lap in a rapid-fire motion, and one leg jiggled in time to the beat.

Bradford's expression was furious. His nostrils flared, and he glanced at the door as if sharing Evie's worries over what Sean might do. Would he come back? Or maybe he'd wait outside the door until they were finished to accost his sister.

Evie had to focus. She had an entire group of book club readers in her shop. She'd already been completely distracted by the fact that the shop was a disaster area, with shelves pushed up against the walls and boxes stacked everywhere, not to mention the multicoloured floor that could trip one of her customers if they weren't paying attention. Her stress levels were high. The last thing she needed was for Sean to cause trouble.

As the rest of the group continued answering the question she'd posed, she did her best to empty her thoughts of all her worries and fix her attention on the person speaking. Her pulse rate began returning to normal, and her smile became more genuine. She could do this — all she had to manage was to get through the evening and go to bed. Everything would look better in the morning—she was certain of it.

Just then, a strange scent drifted to her nostrils. She froze, squeezing the book between her hands until her knuckles grew white. She knew that smell. What was it?

She looked around frantically, hoping to find a clue to help her mind ascertain what she was missing. Panic crept up her spine. The smell made her freeze. It was familiar, and yet the word evaded her grasping consciousness.

"Fire!" she shouted suddenly.

The entire room fell silent as heads swivelled her direction in unison. Then there was pandemonium. People leapt from their seats and rushed for the front door.

Evie jumped onto her chair and raised both hands in the air. "Slow down! Make your way outside carefully and with consideration for the people around you."

She wasn't sure if anyone heard her, but the crowd seemed to comply. She climbed down from the chair and rushed into the café area, squeezing past the barricade. She couldn't see where the fire was located, but smoke wafted high against the ceiling. The fire must be coming from outside. She hurried into the back storage room and collected the important papers she kept in the filing cabinet, then hurried to fill bags with her favourite photo albums, rolls of film, and other sentimental belongings.

David poked his head into the office, where she was scrambling frantically from one cupboard to the next, shoving things into the bags that hung from her forearms. "Can I help?"

She nodded. "Here. Take these."

"You can't stay. The fire has spread. I've called the fireys, but they'll be at least half an hour. Apparently, they're all volunteers who live nearby."

Evie's heart sank. She knew Coral Island's fire department was staffed by volunteers, but that tidbit of trivia had never felt personal until this moment. "There's a hose on the left side of the building. See if it will help."

With a quick nod, David collected the bags and hurried away. Evie filled two more bags, but she had to raise her shirt up over her nose to breathe by that time. She coughed and wheezed, then with one last glance around the bookshop, she ducked out through the front door.

When she got outside, the last of her breath was stolen away by what she saw.

The entire building was ablaze. She had to stumble down the steps past a raging inferno that nipped at her legs and body. The intense heat caused her to gasp. Emily held out her arms, face streaked with tears and soot. Evie fell against her sister, who embraced her with a cry.

"I thought you were going to die. You shouldn't have stayed inside so long."

"I'm sorry," Evie whispered, her throat hoarse. She hadn't realised how close she'd come to disaster. The fire was muted inside, mostly smoke and ash. The outside of the building burned out of control.

She stepped away from her sister, set down the bags on the ground and stared in disbelief as her shop and Bea's café were consumed by flames that leapt and snapped and rose higher with each moment. A few of the men struggled with a tiny hose that sprayed a limp arc of water at the side of the building. The rest of the book club group remained at a distance, watching in horror. People from all over Kellyville arrived in clumps to stare and shake their heads.

Beatrice sidled up to Evie and slipped an arm through hers. She didn't speak. They both stood in silence, gaping at the disaster before them.

"I'm so sorry," David said.

Evie nodded. "Thanks."

"It's going to be okay." Beatrice patted her arm.

"I'm glad everyone got out in time," Evie replied, still unable to process how it had all gone so wrong so fast.

"What happened?" Emily asked, wiping her face with the back of her hand. Streaks of soot smudged across her cheeks.

Charmaine stepped forward. "It was Sean."

"You don't know that," Bea replied with a sympathetic look.

"Yes, we do," Evie countered. "He took a lit candle with him when he left. He was angry."

"I'm sorry," Charmaine said as tears pooled in her eyes. "This is all my fault."

Evie and Bea reached for her in unison. They embraced her as one. "It's not your fault. Don't say that," Bea said.

"Bea's right. This isn't your doing. It's his."

"But he's here because of me," Charmaine sobbed.

"You couldn't know he'd do something like this."

The island's fire engine arrived then, and the volunteer fire brigade got to work extinguishing the flames. It took hours before they were left with a smouldering mess. The rest of the book club had gone home by then. They'd all been examined by paramedics, who arrived soon after the fire engine. Everyone was cleared to leave, and most of them had gone much earlier in the night. Only Evie, Emily, Beatrice and Charmaine remained. The four women huddled in a group, covered in smudges of black soot and with tear-streaked faces as the sun glimmered on the horizon.

"We should get some sleep," Evie said.

Emily nodded. "Come on—let's go home. We can't do anything else now."

Beatrice sighed. "I'll call you later. We can figure out what to do."

"Okay," Evie said. She let herself be led away by Emily. Her heart was a stone in her chest. Her head throbbed, and her eyes were sore from crying. Everything she'd worked so hard to build for so many years was gone. Her dream was over, her livelihood ruined. She had nothing left.

Thirteen

CHARMAINE LAY ON HER BACK, staring up at the ceiling fan overhead. It turned slowly, whirring in a steady rhythm. She'd sweated all over her sheets throughout the day. At least she'd washed off the soot and smoke from the previous night before crashing into bed. She'd left a message for Betsy that she wouldn't be able to work and had spent the day tossing and turning in her small bed. The air-conditioning hadn't successfully fought off the heat of the day, blasting warm air into the room. She needed a new unit, but if she was moving to Bea's cottage, there was no point asking for one.

If she stayed on the island.

After what'd happened the night before, she wasn't sure what to do. Maybe Sean hadn't set the fire. But if he had, what then? She couldn't stay on Coral Island if it meant Sean was a threat to her friends' lives and businesses. He'd possibly burned Bea and Evie's businesses to the ground, and if he was capable of that, what else might he do?

Her mobile phone dinged. She looked to see a message from Bea. Another one. There were a dozen messages that'd arrived throughout the day, people wanting her to call them back, offering support and encouragement. But she couldn't read them or reply. All she felt was guilt and shame.

This was her fault. She should've given Sean the jewellery, or at least reported him to the police. Something to get him off Coral Island. Perhaps she should've left the island the first moment she spotted him in the street outside the café. But she hadn't, and now the café was gone, along with Evie's beautiful little bookshop. The place she'd felt most safe and alive here on the island. The one group of people who'd welcomed her into their lives and given her a reason to hope that the future might be better than her past.

Her phone buzzed again. She shoved it beneath her pillow and swung her legs over the side of the bed. Her hair was matted against her back, her entire body sticky with sweat. She shuffled to the shower and left the water on cold, enjoying the feel of it as it washed her clean again.

With her hair still wet, she dressed quickly and grabbed her camera and a big floppy hat with oversized sunglasses. Maybe she could slip down to the shoreline to take some photographs without being recognised. She had to get out of the flat, but she didn't want to talk to anyone. She had a lot of thinking to do, and in order to make a rational decision, she should clear her head and take a break from the manic spiral going on in her brain. The idea that her presence had caused so much pain to people she'd begun to care about was more than she could handle. It was causing a physical pain in her throat, chest and gut that made her want to cry.

She plodded downstairs to find her bike. Watson was still out. He preferred to be outdoors when it was disgustingly hot. He'd come back home in the evening looking for his dinner and would curl his tail around her leg, purring, until she fixed it for him.

Once she was on her bike, everything began to look better. The world flew by with a few quick pumps of her legs. The sun had begun to drift towards the ocean and the oppressive heat of the day had waned, even if it hadn't shifted inside her flat yet. Seagulls squawked overhead as a pair of pelicans glided towards the dock.

She spent half an hour moving around the dock, photographing the pelicans as they followed fishermen and snapped up fish guts with their enormous beaks. She took pictures of the seagulls diving and squawking as they fought for any remnants, and of the boats as they idled to shore. A pod of dolphins cruised by, sliding through the azure water and playing in the golden light of the setting sun.

"Hi, Chaz," said a small, sweet voice.

Charmaine spun around to find Samantha, Betsy's granddaughter, standing before her in a swimsuit. Her brown hair was wet, and her face had a reddish glow. She held two handfuls of sand up over the beach and was letting the watery substance dribble through her fingers. She'd built a wet sandcastle with dribbles for each pillar, and a large moat that she'd dug around the entire structure and filled with water.

"Hi, Sam. What are you doing there?"

"I'm making the best fortress you've ever seen."

"You certainly are." Charmaine squatted beside the castle and snapped Sam's photo.

"Can I see?"

"Sure." Charmaine showed Sam the picture. She promptly continued building her fortress.

"Are you here by yourself?"

"Dad's over there." She pointed to where her father leaned against a pole, a phone stuck to his ear. He waved to her, then shoved the phone into his pocket and walked over to greet her.

"Hi, Chaz."

"Hello, Frank. It's a nice evening to be at the beach."

"Huh? Oh, yeah. I guess. Listen, is Mum at the shop?"

"Yes, I think so. I wasn't at work today."

"Are you sick?"

"Something like that. I was in town last night..."

"The fire? Yeah, I saw it. Drove past the spot this morning on my way to work. So sad. But I'm glad it didn't spread any further than it did."

She nodded mutely, her throat aching.

"Are you okay?"

"I feel a bit off, but I'm fine otherwise. I'm more worried about Bea and Evie." She wiped her eyes with the back of her hand and pretended she was swatting for flies.

"I wonder what they'll do now," he mused. "I'm going to stop in and see Mum on the way home. Thought she might like to come for dinner."

Charmaine raised a hand over her eyes to cut the afternoon glare. "I think it's good you're making an effort to mend fences."

His face clouded over. "What has Mum told you?"

She blanched. "Oh, nothing. I heard you arguing a couple of times."

He paused, lengthening the silence between them until she thought perhaps she should leave. Then he spoke again. "I guess you heard me calling her a liar, then?"

She nodded slowly. "I'm sorry—I didn't mean to listen in. I was at work, that's all."

"It's fine," he said with a wave of his hand. "You should know who you're working for, I guess."

She sighed. "The thing is, Betsy has always been so good to me."

He laughed hollowly. "She's great to everyone else. Just not to me."

"Really?"

He ran a hand over his face. He suddenly looked much older. "I'm joking. She's a good mother. But it seems like every time I have a relationship with someone, she runs them off.

She has so many secrets, half the time I'm not sure I can trust her at all. The other half of the time, I feel guilty for being mean to her. She acts like she's the perfect mother and grandmother, but she never changes. She says sorry, but then she does it all over again."

Charmaine nudged the sand with her toe. She still didn't know what Frank was talking about, but she supposed she could understand him being upset with Betsy if she was responsible for his wife leaving him. Although, she found that difficult to believe — how could Betsy push Frank's wife away? How could she cause a woman to leave her family behind the way Sam's mother had?

"Do you blame her for your wife leaving?"

He glared at Chaz.

"Sorry, that's probably too personal. You don't have to answer," she stammered.

"It's fine—I don't mind. I've yelled about it loud enough for the entire neighbourhood to hear, so I guess I can explain. When I married my wife, Mum said she wasn't good enough for me and that she'd leave. She explained that my wife didn't understand what it means to be family, how much of a sacrifice it takes to have someone in your life who always has your back, just as you have theirs."

"Did she know her well?" Charmaine asked.

He shrugged. "Not really. I didn't think she knew her at all. But then, five years later, my wife left me. She left Sam, too —that's the worst part. My mother was right, but now I can't figure out if my wife left because Mum knew her so well, or if she left because my mother ran her out of town."

"What did Betsy do?"

"Nothing concrete—not that I could see, anyway. But Rose—that was my wife's name—she told me over and over that she was afraid of Mum, that Mum was mean to her, that she threatened her. I didn't believe her at the time. I mean, you've met Mum — she doesn't have a mean bone in her body. But then she left, and Mum acted as though nothing was wrong. She just went on with her life as usual. Meanwhile, Sam and I were devastated. Our whole lives went up in flames while Mum played pretend. I don't know if what Rose said was true, but I've blamed Mum anyway."

Frank looked so forlorn that Charmaine felt bad for him. He was a large, hulking man, his face covered with greying stubble he never seemed to shave, wearing clothes that were always stained with dirt and grease. He badly needed a haircut, and there were dark smudges beneath his bloodshot eyes.

"I'm sorry, that sounds awful. It's a lot for you to deal with, especially raising..." She glanced at Sam, who was still busy building her sandcastle.

He nodded. "Thanks."

"I know Betsy has been pretty anxious about her brother getting arrested and going to jail."

Frank grunted and crossed his arms.

Charmaine continued. "She's adamant that he's innocent."

Another grunt.

"Do you think he did it?"

Frank's cheeks grew red. "Time to go home, Sam."

"Betsy visited that cave where Bea found the evidence against Buck. Do you know why she went there?"

Frank glared at her. "Cave? My mother? Now you're being ridiculous. She's eighty years old. Come on, Sam. You'll be starving before we make it home if we stay any longer. What do you want for dinner?"

"Spaghetti!" Sam shouted, jumping to her feet. She waved goodbye to Charmaine and dashed off in the direction of the parking lot, her little legs pumping hard.

"I've got to go," Frank said, shoving his hands into the pockets of his baggy shorts. "Nice to see you again, Chaz."

"Okay. Bye."

She watched him stride to the parking lot and put Sam into the car. He clearly didn't want to talk about his uncle, even though he was happy to share personal details about Betsy and his relationship with his former wife. The whole island was talking about Buck Clements and his murder charge. Why wouldn't his nephew want to address the subject? If he thought his uncle was innocent, surely he'd say so. Unless he considered him guilty. Maybe he knew something and didn't want to let any details slip in case Charmaine went to the police.

Fourteen

THE NEXT DAY, Evie walked into Bea's kitchen and set a container of salad on the bench. Bea bustled around the kitchen, marinating chicken. She wore an apron tied around her waist with a picture of a galah on the front and writing that said, *Don't be a galah.*

Galahs were known for their loud, erratic behaviour, something Bea could never be accused of, but Evie often thought of herself as something of a galah. She often wondered if others saw her the same way. She tripped over her words and said the wrong things at the wrong times, and her laughter was high-pitched and often out of place. Yet in her forties, she'd grown to love all those things about herself. She'd matured and become someone who didn't care if strangers thought she was bizarre. Her friends cared about her, and that was what mattered.

But now, with her sister in town and the fire at the bookshop, she felt the ground giving way beneath her feet. All the confidence she'd built in recent years had been shaken, and she didn't have the strength left to build it back up again. She wasn't sure if she'd ever return to that place of contentment and joy.

Bea stopped what she was doing and embraced Evie. "Hi, friend."

"Hi."

They embraced for several long moments. Evie's throat tightened.

"How are you?" Bea asked, pulling back and looking at Evie with concern in her large brown eyes.

Evie pushed a smile across her face. It wobbled. "I'm okay. You?"

"Still in shock, I think. I can't believe all that work..." She stopped speaking and pressed a hand to her mouth. "I spoke to the police today and gave my full statement."

"Me too," Evie replied, recalling the vacillation between intensity and boredom that'd permeated her entire morning at the station.

"It was stressful."

"Definitely," Evie agreed. "It felt like I was under suspicion."

"I know what you mean. Anyway, never mind. That's not why we're here today. We have other things to talk about."

"I'm not sure I'm ready to discuss the fire yet anyway," Evie said. "I'll happily change the subject. Do you know why Penny invited us all to lunch?"

"No idea. I offered to have it at my house because Penny has been so stressed lately. I'm hoping she has good news for us and that this is some kind of celebration because we could all do with some cheering up."

Taya breezed into the kitchen and kissed them both on the cheek. She didn't have a chance to say anything other than offering them condolences about the fire before Penny arrived.

Penny had lost weight. Her cheeks were gaunt, and her clothes hung from her thin frame. She looked scared or sad, or something equally distressing. Evie couldn't figure out what to say, so she simply hugged her friend.

Taya pretended everything was fine, but her face was pale with shock.

Beatrice handed Penny a glass of wine. "Let's all take a seat. I've made some appetisers to get us started — baked camembert with crusty bread, olives and artichoke dip. Also, there's plenty of wine."

"That sounds amazing, Bea. Thanks for doing this," Penny said, taking the wine and leading the way out to the deck.

Aidan and Bea's deck had a stunning outlook over the ocean. A light breeze cut through the humidity. Evie found a seat and poured herself another glass of wine before offering top-ups to the other ladies, who gratefully accepted.

She ate a piece of bread with camembert before speaking. "So, Penny honey. What brings us all together today?"

Penny set down her wine glass. "I've hired someone to manage the refuge."

"What? Why?" Bea asked.

Evie gaped.

Penny gestured for them to wait. "There's more. Rowan has been unhappy, as you all know. He wants to go back to working as a journalist, which means a lot of travel. We're newlyweds, so we obviously don't think it's a good idea for us to be apart. We've decided that we'll travel together and take the opportunity for a kind of extended working honeymoon."

The three friends sat in silence. Evie didn't know what to say. She wanted to be supportive, but the look of anguish on Penny's face was more than she could bear.

"Honey, are you sure about this?" Taya asked, her expression kind.

Penny gave a quick nod. "It's the best thing for us right now."

"But your animals..." Evie began.

"They'll be fine. In fact, I think it's a good thing for me to have a break. I've been working so hard for so long. I haven't had a real holiday in years, besides our honeymoon. This is my chance to have a rest, for us to build our marriage and for Rowan to show me what he does for a living."

"I think it's great," Bea said, her eyes full of sadness.

"Definitely. You're going to love it," Evie added. Penny needed their encouragement—the decision was already made. And besides, she was right. She needed a break.

"I knew Rowan wasn't satisfied working at the refuge, but there must be more to it," Taya added. "You don't have to tell us anything, but you're looking so gaunt."

Taya was worried about Penny. Evie knew her better than anyone, and Evie felt the same way. She didn't want to encourage Penny to leave her support network if Rowan would make her life miserable no matter where they lived.

"I'm fine," Penny replied. "I don't eat when I'm anxious, and having an unhappy husband is stressful. I'm worried we made a mistake getting married so quickly. I feel like I hardly know him. The happy, easygoing man I knew is gone. Instead, I have an irritable bear of a man who hardly speaks to me other than to complain about our lives together. I'm being unfair, I know that. He's not so bad, but it feels that way to me. I'm walking on eggshells all the time."

"That's awful," Evie said, her heart aching. "Are you certain you want to leave the island to spend all your time with him, relying on him for everything?"

"I've got to give it a shot," Penny replied. "If it doesn't work out, I can come home, but I've got to try. We committed our lives to one another. If he's unhappy, I'll do what I can to help him. If I'm unhappy, I hope he'll do the same."

Taya inhaled a sharp breath. "I hate this."

"Me too," Penny said. "But I don't hate the idea of traveling the world with my fancy-pants journalist husband. My dream is that he wakes up from his foul mood and becomes the man I fell in love with all over again."

"Maybe he needs counselling," Bea offered. "It can help sometimes."

"I think that's a great idea. When we're out on the road, I'll suggest it. He might be open to it. I know he's seen a therapist in the past."

"A lot has happened in the past six months," Evie said. "I'm sure you're both feeling a lot of emotions about everything."

"You're right. He won't talk about any of it. I think it's eating away at him," Penny replied, then rubbed her eyes. "I haven't been sleeping well."

"No wonder," Taya replied. "You poor thing."

"We'll be thinking of you," Evie added.

"Yes and you can call us anytime," Bea said.

Penny laughed through a blur of tears. "What would I do without you?"

* * *

On the drive home from Bea's house, Evie listened to some upbeat music and wound the windows down on her four-wheel drive. The wind blew her hair until it was tied in knots while she sang along to the music at the top of her lungs. The lunch with her friends had left her emotionally drained, but strangely uplifted. Being around them reminded her that she wasn't alone, even though it often felt that way.

She cruised past the smouldering ruins of her bookshop and was reminded that she had to call the insurance company among a hundred other tasks that she'd written down on a yellow notepad in her kitchen before she left that morning. It was overwhelming, and she wasn't sure where to begin.

Her phone rang. She turned down the music. "Hello?"

"Hi, Evie. It's Brett here. I thought I'd give you a call since I didn't hear from you this morning."

She slapped a hand to her forehead. She'd forgotten to call her contractor. He didn't know about that the building had been burned to the ground and was still planning on finishing the painting later in the week.

With a clenched stomach she explained to him what had happened. He was thoughtful and kind and expressed his condolences. When they hung up the phone, Evie's good mood was gone. She wound up the windows and slumped down into her seat as she parked in the garage and switched off the engine. Then with a sigh, she climbed out of the car and wandered into the house.

Emily sat on the couch with a cup of tea. "I boiled the kettle if you want a cuppa."

"Thanks." Evie poured herself a cup and joined her sister.

"How were the girls?"

"Penny's going away for a while with Rowan."

"That sounds nice."

"I hope so," Evie replied. She sipped her tea. "What are you planning on doing today?"

"I don't know. I suppose I could help you make some phone calls, if you like."

"That would be great—thanks. I've got a list somewhere." She searched the kitchen and found the list by the toaster, then scanned it. "You could call the book distributors for me. I have their numbers on my phone."

"Happy to help."

"Thanks. I'm glad you're here with me right now. I feel so overwhelmed by it all. I have no idea what I'm going to do with my life."

Emily sighed. "I know what you mean."

"What's going on with you?" Evie asked. "You haven't

told me much, but I have to assume you're dealing with some issues or you wouldn't be here."

Emily scowled. "My husband doesn't love me."

"What? Of course he does. He's always loved you. He's just not great at showing it sometimes."

Emily's face reddened. "Don't tell me about my own husband. You think you know him better than I do, but you don't. I've lived with the man for ten years. He's helped me raise my boys. We've been a family for a long time."

Evie swallowed a mouthful of tea. It scalded her throat. She coughed. "That's ridiculous. I don't think I know him better than you, but I do know him pretty well. He was my boyfriend before he was yours, after all."

Emily's nostrils flared. "How dare you bring that up again."

"Why not? I think enough time has passed that we can finally discuss what happened. After all, it ruined my life."

"Ruined your life? You want Gareth Johnson so badly, you're welcome to him. I can't stand him." Emily strode to the kitchen, where she threw the rest of her tea into the sink.

Evie followed her, rage building slowly up her spine. "What do you mean, you can't stand him? What's going on, Emily?"

Emily pressed both hands to the edge of the sink. "It's pointless. I've tried to win his love and affection for such a long time, but it's still you. He's always loved you. I know that now."

"We were trying to get pregnant. We wanted to be married and spend our lives together. We lived in the same house for eight years, Emily. And you stole him from me with your flirting and your promises." Evie choked out the words as a lump grew in her throat at the memory. She'd built her entire life around a man who gave her up for her sister. It'd derailed her, thrown her entirely off course. She'd never married, never had a family of her own. Emily had taken all of that from her. She'd finally recovered on Coral Island and now Emily was back, reopening old wounds.

Emily's eyes sparked with anger. "I didn't steal anything. He came to me."

"That's not true."

"Why does any of this matter now?" Emily threw her hands in the air.

"Because you're doing it again. You knew David was going to ask me out, and you stepped in between us. You've been seeing him for weeks, and once again, I'm out in the cold alone."

"You didn't seem to care. You didn't say anything to me about it."

Evie slumped back onto the couch. "Because it wouldn't make a difference. We've been here before. You're going to do whatever you want to do, and you don't care how it makes me feel."

"That's unfair, Evie. You always ignore my feelings because yours are just so much more important. Mum and Dad do it too. Because I'm too emotional and dramatic, all three of you have ganged up on me my whole life. I'm miserable and alone, my own husband prefers my sister, my kids are ungrateful, and I've got no one." Emily burst into tears, covering her face with both hands.

Evie's resolve wavered. She didn't have any fight left. Would Emily ever own up to the things she'd done or take responsibility for her own actions? "I'm sorry. I didn't realise you felt that way. I suppose it does seem like we gang up on you sometimes."

The truth was, she'd taken refuge in her parents' support. Emily had always been so strong-willed that Evie often felt bulldozed by her sister. Her only defence had been to run to her parents for words of affirmation and encouragement. She hadn't realised the impact that might have on Emily's self-esteem and sense of family.

"Thanks for finally admitting it." Emily sniffled.

"I'm happy to admit my part. But the truth is, you never give me a chance to be the kind of sister I want to be. Your jealousy and impulsive behaviour are hurtful. You need to take responsibility for the things you've done. I can't forgive you until you do that. I can't move on."

Tears glistened in Emily's eyes. Her cheeks grew bright red. "You always blame me."

Evie's rage returned like a fire in her belly. "Because it's your fault!"

"It's not just me, Evie. You..."

"No, it *is* just you, Em. I didn't contribute to any of it. Yes, maybe I took Gareth for granted. Maybe I wasn't there for you when you needed me. Maybe I sometimes rubbed things in your face. But these are normal relationship things. They're not the same as betraying your only sister and stealing her long-term boyfriend."

Evie retreated to the back veranda, she sat in a rocking chair and gazed over the garden. A fly buzzed around Evie's nose, and she swatted it away. Bees hummed around the flowers. The heat pushed up against her as if attempting to bully her back into the house. She drew deep breaths to calm the rage that made her want to scream and cry, to stamp and yell. There was no point. It was all in the past. Nothing to be done about any of it.

Emily stepped through the back door, her nose and eyes reddened. "Is that how you feel about me?" She sat in the rocking chair beside Evie's.

Evie's head throbbed and her throat ached. If only her sister would hear her words for the first time and realise what she'd done. "Yes, it's how I feel. Finally. It's taken me this long to express it, but I can't keep it to myself any longer. You're in my house, accepting my help and hospitality. I'm not going to be your doormat any longer. You say you're sorry, or you can leave. For good."

Emily blinked. "I'm sorry. You know I am."

"You've never told me that," Evie replied, her eyes brimming with tears. "Not once in all these years."

Emily faced her with a sob. "I am sorry. I shouldn't have pursued Gareth, not while you were in a relationship with him. I've had to live with that mistake for most of my life. I couldn't walk away from him because I felt so guilty about taking him from you. I went through with a wedding I didn't want and raised a family with a man I knew didn't love me."

"Why did *he* go through with it?" Evie asked. She'd always wondered this, but they'd never been able to have an honest conversation without shouting words of condemnation and acrimony.

"I think he felt guilty as well. Looking back, I can see that he knew early on he'd made a mistake. But he couldn't undo it, didn't know how to make it right. He took to drinking soon after we were married, and it's only gotten worse over the years."

"That must be hard on you," Evie replied, her voice soft. The emotion that'd built up, like a row of bricks on her shoulders that she'd carried around for so long, began to fall away.

Emily nodded. "I don't know what to do. I thought dating David might help, but all it did was made me feel worse."

"Dating another man is definitely not the way to work out your marriage problems. Especially when it's basically repeating the same mistake over again. You knew I liked him and that he liked me. Yet you stepped in between us, just like you did with Gareth."

Emily pressed both hands to her face and sobbed, her

body shaking. "I know. I'm sorry. I don't know why I act like this. Truly, I don't. I've ruined everything."

Evie breathed in deep, inhaling the comforting scent of summer in the air. "It seems both of us have missed out on a wonderful sisterly relationship all these years because of some big mistakes. I hope we're able to put it all behind us and move forward."

"I hope so too. Can you ever forgive me?"

Evie searched within herself for the answer. The pain in her heart was gone, and the burden on her shoulders had toppled. She felt light—empty, but otherwise good. "Yes, I can finally forgive you. But you've got to stop repeating the same mistakes."

Emily wiped her nose again. Her eyes were red-rimmed, her neck blotchy. "I want to be different. I really do."

"Then you've got to go home and talk to Gareth."

Emily nodded. "I know."

"It's not going to be easy, but he does love you. It might not seem like it sometimes, but he does. He's your husband and he chose you. You need to treat him right, and communicate. He was never good at talking. He's flawed, but he still deserves better than the way you've treated him."

Emily sighed. "Yes, you're right. I've felt so guilty about what I did to you that I didn't fight for our marriage. Not really."

Evie leaned back in her chair and closed her eyes. "You were young and stupid. I don't envy your marriage—not anymore. I haven't for years."

"Will we ever move past this?" Emily asked, her gaze searching Evie's face. "Please, I don't have anyone. You're my family."

Emily was always so dramatic. She couldn't see the good things in front of her. "You're not alone. You've got me, our parents, your sons and your husband."

"I don't have Gareth. Not anymore. I've ruined what we had."

"You need to forgive yourself and go back to Gareth, if you still care about your marriage — talk to him. Work things out."

"I don't know if he'll listen."

"He will if you give him a chance. Don't storm out or make a big dramatic statement. Go to him, show him you care, listen to him."

"I don't make big dramatic statements," Emily replied with a huff.

Evie grinned. "Uh huh."

"You always think the worst of me."

"Then prove me wrong. Fix your marriage and appreciate your family. Enjoy your life, and stop looking for ways to sabotage yourself and everyone around you. You're better than that. You deserve better than that."

Emily hugged Evie. "Thank you."

They cried together for a while, then Emily returned to her room to pack her bags. She was going home, and Evie would have the house to herself again. What she would do with her life then, she had no idea.

Fifteen

CHARMAINE WAS RIDING her bike down Main
Street when she saw Sean. She hadn't seen him since the fire
and hoped he'd skipped town. He wore a pair of board shorts
and a cap, but no shirt. He was tanned and fit, licking an ice
cream and watching her approach. There was no chance he
hadn't seen her. She slowed the bike and stepped off, heart
pounding in her chest.

"What are you still doing here?" she asked.

He laughed. "Why would I go anywhere else? I love it
here."

"You burned the café and the bookshop to the ground.
I'm calling the police."

"I didn't touch them, and you can't prove otherwise,"
Sean hissed, stepping closer with a menacing look on his face.

"Just go," she said. "Leave. You don't belong here. It's not
fair to do this to people who've done nothing to hurt you."

"I'm here for you and for the jewellery."

"What is this jewellery you keep talking about?" She knew
what he was referring to, but she still didn't understand where
it'd come from or how he knew about it. She'd found it in a

small portable safe in her mother's room after her death. Charmaine had spent several weeks cleaning out cupboards and selling furniture in preparation for the renters to move in. She'd stumbled on the cache of diamond jewellery by accident, along with the combination in a pocket of her mother's purse.

How had Mum got hold of such expensive items? She assumed they were expensive, but hadn't checked with a professional. Instead, she'd simply put them away to think about at another time. But since Sean was so interested in finding the pieces, clearly they were worth more than she'd realised.

"You know what I'm talking about. I'm guessing you found the necklace and tennis bracelet. Didn't you?"

"I don't know what you mean..." Charmaine's heart raced.

He snarled. "I know all about them. Mum told me when she was close to the end. Said they were worth millions. They're mine too, and I want them. I'm sticking around until you hand them over. It would be a shame if the florist shop suffered a similar fate to the café. I'm sure you'd agree."

She gasped, her eyes wide. "Don't you dare."

"Give me the necklace."

Her thoughts raced. What would it take to get rid of him? She didn't want to hand over the jewellery, but maybe that was her only play.

"I don't have the jewellery. Mum was delusional. If I had something worth millions, I wouldn't be living in this hovel and working two minimum wage jobs. Would I?"

Doubt flitted through his eyes. "If you don't have them, where are they?"

"I have no idea. How much money do you owe, anyway?"

He told her the amount and she swallowed hard, frantically trying to think of a way to get her brother to leave town once and for all.

"I'll call the solicitor and find out if I can withdraw any

more money from the mortgage on Mum's house. If I can get enough to pay your debts, will you leave me and my friends alone?"

He shrugged. "Can you do that?"

"I don't know, but I can try."

"It's a start."

There was something so irritating about the smug look on Sean's face. She wanted to slap it off, but she'd never been violent in her life. Her instinct was usually to run. She wasn't sure where the anger came from, but it gave her confidence.

"Fine. I'll see what I can do. But if I manage this, I want you to leave Coral Island and never come back."

He laughed out loud. "I'm going to need more than that. Give me the keys to Mum's house. I want to look for that jewellery."

"I can't give you the keys—someone's living there. If you break in, the police will nab you for sure. They're already looking for you over the bookshop fire."

"I had nothing to do with that," he spat, eyes flashing.

"If that's true, I guess you won't mind them asking you questions."

"Not a chance. The hicks in this town would frame me for sure."

* * *

By the time she reached the solicitor, who'd been out to lunch the first time she called, Charmaine had chewed through every single one of her fingernails. She sat on the couch, fingers drumming on the fabric, while she thought about her next step.

The solicitor had said it was up to the bank whether they'd allow her to take out another mortgage. The bank told her the loan was already set up to allow withdrawals up to a limit, so she could take what she needed. It was all much easier than she'd thought it would be. And now she had a cashier's cheque in her purse, ready for her meeting with Sean.

She figured she owed him the money anyway — it was partly his inheritance. He'd left town before collecting, and her mother had given Charmaine power of attorney and the details of her bank accounts. If she paid Sean his portion of the inheritance, partly in a lump sum and then in a monthly stipend to entice him to stay away from her, it might just work.

When she'd asked the solicitor about the jewellery, he'd known nothing about it. The bank had assured her there was no safe deposit box in her mother's name in their paperwork now or in the past. Charmaine had hoped to discover where they'd come from but the solicitor had been no help and neither had the bank.

She had no intention of ever selling the items. Even though she wasn't sure where Mum had gotten them, or what they'd meant to her, they'd clearly meant something or she would've used them long ago to pay off their debts and to give them a better lifestyle.

With her purse tucked firmly beneath her arm, she headed for the Thai restaurant downstairs. She'd arranged to meet Sean there in an hour, but she wanted to get a seat early and calm her nerves with a Mai Tai cocktail before she had to face him. She found a table near the back of the restaurant so she could watch the door, then hunched over her phone while she waited for her drink.

Bea came through the front door and strode to the back of the restaurant with Aidan, Harry, Dani and a man Charmaine didn't recognise trailing behind her.

"Chaz, I wasn't expecting to see you here. I thought you'd be working," Beatrice said.

"Mum, it's too hot for Thai food," Dani complained. She

held hands with the man Charmaine didn't know. He looked to be about twice Dani's age. He had grey streaks in his dark curls, and his brown eyes were small and close set.

"You always say that and then you love it," Bea replied. "Let's get that table." She pointed to one across from Charmaine, then sat down opposite her. "I'm going to sit with you for a minute while they decide what they want to eat. It can be a bit of an ordeal to order when we all go out together."

"It must be nice to have Dani and Harry home for a little while."

"They'll be back at university in Sydney in no time. The summer holidays have gone quickly this year, since they both worked for much of the time."

"Who's the man with Dani?"

Bea's lips formed a thin, straight line. She inhaled a quick breath. "That's Damien, her architecture lecturer."

"Oh, that's right, I recall you mentioning that she was dating an older man. How's that going?"

"According to Dani, it's amazing."

"And how do you feel?"

Bea turned her head away from the group and whispered. "I'm not so keen, but I'm working on acceptance and support."

Charmaine laughed. "You're doing great."

"Thank you." Bea dipped her head. "And how about you? Just having some lunch on your own?"

"I've taken a few days off work to deal with some personal issues. I'm meeting Sean here for lunch in a little while."

"That's big of you. Aren't the police looking for him?"

"They want to talk to him about the fire, along with everyone else who was there that night. I've told him that he needs to go into the station to make a statement."

Bea's eyes narrowed. "Do you think he will?"

"I don't know. I'll mention it again today." Charmaine

had to walk a fine line with her friendships. She hated for Bea to think Sean might've had something to do with the fire at her café, but the truth was, Charmaine didn't know. She couldn't believe he would do something so destructive, but then she'd been wrong about him before on countless occasions. If she reported him to the police, he might end up in prison. Perhaps he was right — the local cops might frame him. They'd framed Betsy's brother—at least, that was the story according to Betsy.

"I have good news," Bea said suddenly, changing tack.

"I'd love to hear it."

"Harry got into the medicine program at uni. He'll be studying it next year."

Charmaine grinned. "That's amazing. I'm so happy for him—and for you."

"He knew what he wanted to do with his life when he was a small child. Now it's finally happening. I'm so proud of him."

"You should be proud. That's a big achievement."

Beatrice returned to her table to order. There was a lot of back-and-forth and raised voices as they negotiated on dishes to share. Charmaine listened in silence as she scrolled through news items on her phone, a smile on her face. No matter how much they might argue, Bea's family was the kind of family Charmaine longed to one day have for herself.

She read through the headlines. There were several articles about the fire — all of them were short and to the point. None of them mentioned any suspects. It seemed the police hadn't yet released information about whether there was foul play involved. So, it could've been electrical—she hoped it was. If Sean had been responsible, she wasn't sure she could live with the guilt of having brought him to the island.

He showed up fifteen minutes late in a strange mood. He

slumped into the chair opposite Charmaine, but kept glancing over his shoulder at the door.

"Can we switch?" he asked.

She nodded. "Fine. Are you expecting company?"

"I hope not," he replied as they shifted seats.

When he was facing the door, he relaxed more while they ordered their food. Charmaine felt warm and relaxed from the Mai Tai. She watched her brother fidget and itch, shift and swallow as he placed his order. He was frightened. She'd never seen him like this before.

"Do you have my money?"

She patted her handbag. "I need to talk to you first."

Charmaine continued. "I'll give you this money—it's your portion of the inheritance. Well, some of it — enough to cover your debts. The rest, I will deposit monthly into your bank account if you promise to stay away from me forever. Think of it as a kind of restraining order. I pay you to keep your distance. You can't return to Coral Island, and you can't follow me anywhere else I choose to go. Otherwise, I stop the payments."

"How did you manage that?"

She sighed. "I took the rest of the equity out of the house. But it's in my name, and from now on, you have no claim to it. I've got a document here for you to sign, then I'll give you the money and we can say goodbye."

His frown was replaced by an easy smile. "Come on, sis. You don't want to do that. You'll miss me. I know you will."

"Maybe someday, but for now, I need you gone. You say you didn't have anything to do with the fire, but I'm not sure I believe you. I don't want you around. You're a troublemaker —you always have been. I don't know why I never realised that growing up. I looked up to you, thought you were the best big brother I could ask for. But now I know better — you've never cared about anyone other than yourself."

His smile faded. "That's not nice."

"Sorry, but you've pushed me to this. I didn't want a confrontation, but here we are."

"We're still family, you and me. We've got no one else."

"You're right. I'll try to be kind."

She'd lived with him long enough to know how to calm his temper and distract him from whatever was bothering him. It didn't always work, but she'd learned to deal with him from a young age. His tendency to fly into a rage had contributed to her proclivity for seeking solitude and quiet. She found it stressful to manage his shifting moods, but she could if she was forced to.

They ate together, chatting about old times. It was as though nothing had gone wrong between them. Sean was a chameleon — able to shift and adjust his mood based on what was going on around him or who he was speaking to. He'd gotten his way, and he no longer had any need to be angry at her.

After his last bite of green curry, he signed the papers and took the money.

"Goodbye, sis. I guess I won't be seeing you anytime soon."

"Goodbye, Sean. Make good choices. Okay?"

He laughed and kissed her cheek before walking out of the restaurant. Charmaine hadn't realised how tense she was until he was gone. She let out a long, slow breath and leaned her elbows on the table in relief. It was over. She'd done it. He was gone, perhaps for good.

She folded the paper to add to her purse, paid the bill, and waved goodbye to Beatrice and Aidan. Then she stepped outside with her face raised towards the sun. She spun in a circle, arms outstretched. For the first time in a long time, she was free.

Sixteen

EVIE WANDERED through the blackened remnants of the bookshop. It was a shell of a structure. She wore protective clothing and a mask. There was no one else around, and for the first time since the fire a week earlier, she was alone in her former place of business. Up until that moment, there'd been insurance adjusters, police investigators, fire inspectors, Janice and other staff, and more. Always someone tramping around her bookshop. She'd answered their questions as best she could, but now she was on her own, and the silence felt overwhelming.

The brand-new bookshelves she'd bought, in solid timber, the ones she'd thought would last forever, were falling apart and entirely black. They were unrecognisable. Her darkroom had been partially destroyed, although some of the filing cabinets had miraculously made it through unharmed, and she'd been able to save files of photographs and negatives she'd developed over the years.

But everything else was gone.

All her work, the years of her life she'd dedicated to this passion of hers—nothing remained. The insurance company

143

had decided that the fire was accidental, since they hadn't been able to identify a cause. They'd assured her she would receive a large payout, as would her landlord. It would be enough money for her to rebuild the business, if that's what she wanted to do.

She stepped outside and slipped off her mask, then lowered herself onto the blackened step. The steel pelican remained, no longer rust-coloured — now black like everything else around her.

"What a disaster," Bradford said as he climbed out of his truck in front of the bookshop.

"Hi, Brad."

He nodded and sat beside her. "I'm sorry, Evie."

"Thanks." She leaned her head against his shoulder.

"What will you do now? Are you going to start all over again?"

She sighed. "I don't know. I was in the middle of a renovation. I'd bought new furniture, we were halfway through painting . . . It was a lot of work. And now..."

"It's gone," he finished.

"Yep. And I'm tired."

"But everyone loves your bookshop."

"I wish they'd loved it enough to shop there." She offered a bitter laugh.

He patted her hand. "Famous last words of every person who opened a business."

"I'm joking... kind of. I had plenty of tourists come through, of course. And sometimes we thrived. But there were days when I wasn't sure we were going to make it. I loved the bookshop too, but I don't want to use the payout to rebuild it. I don't think I like the idea of owning a bookshop anymore. I'm feeling defeated right now."

"It's a great location," Bradford said.

She nodded. "I know. The landlord lives on the mainland,

though, and I haven't been able to reach him. I don't know what he wants to do with the place. He may not want to rebuild, in which case this whole decision is pointless. I can't redo a bookshop where there's no building."

"I wonder if he'd be willing to sell." Bradford glanced around, taking in their surroundings. The bookshop had sat on the corner of the main street, close to the docks and in the centre of the busiest part of town.

"I can't buy it," Evie replied despondently.

"I might, though," Bradford said.

"What?"

"Only if you don't want to redo the bookshop. I'm looking for a second location for my business — we rent yachts and fishing boats out to tourists, and we've outgrown the Airlie Beach location. I want to find somewhere on the island where I can set up an office that will provide scuba diving, snorkelling tours on the reef, boat hire and so on. I also want someone to run a photography outfit as well. Tourists love that kind of thing."

"It's a great idea," Evie mused.

"If you're rebuilding, I'll find another location. But if you don't want to run a bookshop anymore, maybe you could come work for me. I pay a good salary, and you'd have plenty of flexibility. You could run the office, do the bookings, and take the photos. It'd be a small operation at first, so you'd be managing it alone. But I'm hoping it would grow over time and we could hire help."

Evie pondered his words. It wasn't a bad idea. It might be just what she needed. But giving up the bookshop space wasn't something she was ready to do.

"Thanks, Bradford. It means a lot to me that you'd want me to be part of your business. I'll talk to my landlord and think about it. Can I get back to you?"

He grinned. "Yes, please think about it. We'd be great together."

His positivity was contagious. She felt hope stir in the pit of her gut. Maybe her future wasn't so dim. Perhaps she could reinvent herself again. She'd done it before.

* * *

After Bradford left, Evie pushed herself to her feet with a groan. She'd spent days sorting through the ruins of her bookshop. Every part of her body ached, and every muscle was tired and sore. One more hour of it and she'd head home. The house was quiet now, with Emily gone. She'd called when she made it home safely to Emerald. She seemed calmer and more at peace with her lot in life. Their talk had given both of them a sense of release after so many years of tension. They could move on and embrace the lives they'd built for themselves without animosity or jealousy. The anger was gone, and instead, a warm affection remained in its place.

She had her sister back. Even if nothing else worked out in her life, at least she had Emily. She hadn't realised just how much she needed that reconciliation until she had it. She felt like a different person to the one she'd been before. Her anxiety about what the future held had dimmed to a vague sense of discomfort.

"I'm sorry about the fire." When David spoke, it startled her. She'd been so deep in her reverie, she hadn't seen him cross the street from the primary school.

She pressed her hands to her hips and met his gaze. "Thanks."

"You doing okay?"

She shrugged. "I am, which is basically a miracle."

"Do you know what happened yet?" His dark eyes brimmed with compassion. "How did the fire start?"

"We're not sure. The forensic team said that their findings were inconclusive."

"That's frustrating."

He leaned against the railing. His brown hair was combed back in waves away from his face. His skin was more tanned than it'd been when he first arrived.

"Did Emily call you before she left?" It was the last thing she wanted to discuss with David, but knowing her sister as well as she did, it was a necessary conversation to have.

His eyes widened. "Left? Where did she go?"

Evie sighed. In the past, she would've been angry at her sister, but now she simply felt sadness for David. "I'm sorry, David. She went back home. To her husband."

"Her husband?" His brow furrowed. "She's married?"

"She should've told you." Evie ran her fingers through her hair. "But yes, she's married. She has been for almost two decades. She and her husband were having troubles, so she came to stay with me for a little while. Now she's gone back home to try to work things out. I'm afraid you were caught in the crosshairs."

"Oh." He crossed his arms. "Where's home?"

"Emerald — central Queensland. Her husband works for a mining company. She has two adult children as well, although they don't live at home any longer."

"Wow. She didn't mention any of that to me. We had about four dates—I would've thought something like that might come up."

"Again, I'm sorry. She's a unique person, my sister." Evie cleared her throat. "We've been estranged for a number of years, but we're making amends."

"I'm glad you're working it out. As far as she and I go, I'd already told her that I didn't think we had a future together. Four dates was enough. She's a little more than I can handle." His eyes twinkled.

Evie laughed. "She's more than any of us can handle."

"So, the two of you are nothing alike, then?"

"We're complete opposites," Evie replied.

"But you look exactly the same."

"We're twins."

"That's what tripped me up," he continued. "I came over here to ask you out and I thought she was you. I thought you'd just dyed your hair. So I asked Emily out, and she said yes. When I realised she wasn't you, it was too late. I couldn't back out then—it would've been rude. Anyway, I came over here to apologise to you for that. I thought you and I had a spark between us, and I messed the whole thing up."

"It's okay. It's not the first time she's done it. She likes to go after the men I'm interested in."

"Really?"

"Her husband was my boyfriend first. She has a tendency to want what I have, or in your case, what I might someday have. She gets jealous of me, for some reason. I tell her it's pointless to be jealous of your identical twin, but she does anyway."

"Wow. That must've been hard for you," David said, moving closer. He raised a foot to the step below where Evie stood.

He was so close, she could reach out and touch him. She'd admired him from a distance while he dated her sister and had done everything she could not to get jealous, not to wish for something she couldn't have. He was off-limits. She had no desire to be like Emily and pine for something her sister had. But now that Emily was gone, those feelings had returned.

"It was hard for a long time. But then I moved back to Coral Island and set up my bookshop." She waved a hand at the blackened ruins behind her. "You see how well that turned out."

He took another step closer until he was almost touching her. "So, you were interested in me?"

"Um... did I say that?"

"Yes, you did." He laced his fingers through hers, sending a tingle of excitement up her arm.

"I suppose I did."

He leaned towards her, his lips pulled into a teasing half grin. "I'm interested in you as well."

Her stomach did a flip. Then he kissed her, and she forgot everything but the feel of his mouth on hers. He cupped her cheek with his hand and gently pushed his fingers up into her hair. She let herself drift into his arms as her head swam with desire. It was more than she'd expected.

She'd long ago given up hope of finding someone like David. When he'd taken her sister out on a date, she'd packed that piece of her heart away in a box and set it aside. It'd been easy to do—she was used to pushing it away from herself. But now that part of her was wide awake and hungry for more. She stood on tiptoe and laced her arms around his neck, pulling him closer still.

Seventeen

THE NEWSPAPER ARTICLES splayed across the table in front of Charmaine made her cross-eyed. She stared at them until the words no longer made any sense. She'd promised Bea and Penny that she'd look over the articles, but now that they were in front of her, she wasn't sure what to think.

The woman who'd run from the law in California could've been Betsy. The photos of her were old, in black and white, and the young woman in them had a vague similarity to the pictures Betsy used to have on the walls around the back of the florist shop. Since she'd removed the images from their prime position behind the cash register, Charmaine couldn't hold the articles up next to them to compare. Instead, she had to try to remember how they'd looked. She should've taken pictures of them with her phone. Instead, she squinted at the articles and held them up to look from different angles. It was all too hard.

With a sigh, she pushed one article aside and reached for another. They'd either been photocopied from the microfiche files they'd discovered at the library or were printouts of articles she'd found online. It would've been simple to accept the excitement and intrigue of uncovering a conspiracy about her boss where Betsy played the role of an international criminal, but this wasn't a game, and Betsy was a friend. She hated the idea of exposing her as someone who'd run from a marriage more than fifty years ago, but was still wanted by law enforcement on the other side of the globe.

If this woman was Betsy, maybe she had good reason to run. How would exposing her help anyone? And if she wasn't Betsy, the innuendo might spread throughout the community, and Charmaine had seen how rumours could destroy someone's reputation. Her own mother had suffered through enough rumours over the years — the single mother from out of town no one knew anything about and who kept mostly to herself. The local busybodies had nothing to work with, and so they had concocted their own stories about the Billings family. It'd been hard for Mum to ignore, but she'd done her best to stay positive.

The florist shop was silent as dusk settled over the island. Charmaine moved to flick on the lights so she could see better. She pulled blinds down over the windows for privacy. Then she returned to her task, seated on a stool with one foot resting against the table leg.

"Why did you leave your home and husband behind, Betsy?" she asked the grainy printout of a photograph held in her hands.

A loud banging on the front door of the shop startled her. Her heart thudded against her rib cage as she leapt to her feet with a cry. Then, smoothing her hair back with both hands, she hurried to the door and pulled the blind aside to look through the glass into the darkened street.

Frank Norton, Betsy's son, stood there in a pair of jeans and a short-sleeved shirt that was half untucked. His hair was wildly splayed out over his head as though he'd been caught under a lawn mower, and his socks were mismatched.

Charmaine opened the door. "Frank, how are you?"

He grunted. "Fine. Is Sam ready to go?"

"I'm sorry, Frank. She's already gone home with Betsy. I thought she would've called you."

"My phone went dead. It's fine—I'll head off then."

He turned to leave, then spun back again. "Do you mind checking to see if Sam remembered her homework? She often leaves it in the back room and doesn't have it for school the next day."

Charmaine nodded and left the door ajar. "I'll go and look. Won't be a moment."

Frank followed her inside and shut the door behind him. The hairs on the back of Charmaine's neck bristled, but she ignored them. Frank wasn't a danger to her. She breathed deeply, calming the anxiety that tickled the pit of her gut.

A quick check of the back room showed no sign of homework. She stepped back into the shop to find Frank standing next to the table where the articles lay exposed. He wasn't looking down, though. Instead, his gaze was firmly fixed on Charmaine's face. She felt a sudden urge to hustle him out of the shop as quickly as possible. There was something unnerving about him that she'd always ignored, but now it was making her uncomfortable.

"No homework. She must've remembered to take it with her," Charmaine trilled as she headed for the door.

She pulled it open and held it for him. He stepped through and out into the street. "Thanks. I'll see you later then."

When he walked away, Charmaine shut and locked the door behind him, then leaned against it with a giant sigh of relief. She'd been so jumpy since her brother first came to town, she'd become entirely paranoid. What did she think would happen? Frank might be a mess, but he'd never given any indication he might harm her. Yet her instincts had set off alarm bells from the moment she answered the door. She'd become a basket case if she didn't pull herself together soon.

If he'd seen the articles on the table, he'd given no indication. Even if he had, would he make anything of them? Still, she should put them away. It'd been foolish to leave them out in the open in the middle of the shop, even if she was the only one there. He might've seen them and told Betsy what she was doing. But then again, the articles might not have anything to do with Betsy, in which case neither Frank nor Betsy would care about them.

She was so confused. Her thoughts spun around and around in circles. She kept returning to the same ground, thinking through the same scenarios, asking the same questions. It was too much. She had to stop. She was becoming obsessive, and it was likely that her fixation was a result of feeling unsafe over Sean's presence on the island. But as far as she knew, he was gone now. She could move on and forget he'd even been there. Her life was her own to begin again. She should focus her attention on moving to the beach cottage and living the life she'd always dreamed of with Bradford by her side.

Yes, Bradford was the person she should be fixing her thoughts on. A smile drifted across her features as she shuffled the articles into a folder and carried them upstairs to her flat, switching the lights off as she went.

Upstairs, Watson waited patiently, scratching at the door. She let him in and opened a can of cat food to put into his bowl. He ate while watching her, tail tucked around his plump grey body.

"It must be nice to have such a simple life. Go where you like, sleep all day, people feed you, chase a lizard, sleep again, then repeat." She laughed and scratched the top of his head.

Her phone dinged, and she lifted it from her pocket to read a text from Watson's owner, Finn.

Do you know where Watson is?

She responded.

He's here with me. Eating his dinner.

Do you mind if I come and get him? We're heading out of town for a few days, and we have a pet sitter I want him to meet.

No worries.

Charmaine explained to Finn where she lived, then poured herself a glass of juice and ate a peach while she waited.

"I'm finally going to meet the woman who owns you. She's an artist, apparently. A pretty good one. I should probably get changed—I look a mess. But then again, she'll no doubt arrive while I'm naked and I'll trip over my own pants trying to get to the door and knock myself out on the floor, or something equally ridiculous. I hate social anxiety. Know what I mean?"

Watson chewed his food, a blank expression on his face.

"Yeah, I don't think you struggle with it the same way I do, for some reason."

She reached down to scratch behind his ears with a sigh. With everything that'd been going on lately, Charmaine missed her mother more than she had in years. She went looking for her purse and pulled out the photograph of the two of them she kept tucked inside her wallet. The image brought tears to her eyes. She dashed them away with the back of her hand and set about looking for tissues.

There was usually a box on the kitchen bench, but she must've run out. She looked in the drawers by her bed—no tissues to be found. Under the sink, she discovered a new box and was opening it when there was a knock on the back door. She quickly blew her nose as she walked to the door and flung it open.

A woman stood there, bathed in the faint golden light emitting from the outdoor bulb that hung above the staircase.

"Hi, I'm Finn. I'm here about Watson. You must be Chaz."

Charmaine's heart stopped. Her breath caught in her throat, and she stared without blinking.

"Um... Chaz?" The woman's eyes registered confusion. "I have the right place, don't I?" She glanced around, probably looking for a street number or any kind of identifying features in the small flat.

"Oh, there you are, Watson. Come on, boy. You're such a freeloader." The woman stepped into the flat and reached down to pick Watson up. She held him aloft, stroking his head. He folded himself easily into her embrace.

Finn had light golden-brown hair flecked with gray. It was cut short and combed back from her face. She had an enormous cowlick over the left side of her forehead, and her grey eyes twinkled as she spoke to the cat. Her button nose bobbed slightly with each word. She wore a pair of brown linen pants and a white singlet top with a chunky azure necklace around her sun-kissed neck.

Charmaine couldn't speak. She couldn't breathe. Every part of her was poised for—what, she didn't know.

"Um... hi," she finally said.

The woman looked up in surprise. "I was going to ask, 'Cat got your tongue?' But I wasn't sure you'd see the humour in it. Are you okay, honey?"

Tears returned quickly to Charmaine's eyes, and she took slow, tentative steps towards Finn and Watson. "I'm fine. I... thanks for letting me take care of Watson sometimes."

"Oh, that's okay by me. You're doing me a favour. This big sook was so torn up about the new dog, he stayed away for weeks on end. He's finally coming home, but he sits up high as he can away from the puppy on tree branches or the windowsill. I have to admit, though, the pup is a bit vivacious. I can understand Watson's reservations about the relationship."

Charmaine attempted a smile, but she could barely see through a veil of tears.

"Are you sure you're okay? You look like you're about to cry. You don't have to tell me about it, of course, but I'm here if you need someone to talk to."

Tears dropped down Charmaine's cheeks. "It's just that... I don't know how to say this. But you remind me of someone."

"I do? That's nice. I think it's such a compliment when people say things like that. Clearly, it's someone you care about." Finn reached out and squeezed Charmaine's arm gently. "I'm sorry, honey. Whatever it is, I'm sorry."

"She was my mother. She died three years ago, and I've been missing her lately. And one of the reasons I came to Coral Island was to find her sister, my aunt. I don't know if that's you, but you look exactly like her. I mean, not exactly, but you've got the same nose and the same coloured eyes. And your face shape..."

Finn's face grew pale. She gaped. "Charmaine?"

"Yes, Chaz is short for Charmaine."

"You're Helen's daughter?"

"That's right. And you must be her sister." Charmaine laughed and sobbed at the same time.

Finn gently put Watson on the floor, then threw her arms around Charmaine with a shout of joy. "I can't believe it. I thought I'd never see you again. Look at how grown up you are!"

* * *

Charmaine and Finn sat on the couch in the little flat together, Watson in Charmaine's lap, for the next two hours and talked nonstop about everything. Their conversation flowed smoothly and without direction, going back and forth and around, covering every topic that came to mind in a haphazard and joyous fashion.

Charmaine told Finn that her mother had died. Finn cried silently for ten minutes, rocking back and forth on the couch with her hands over her face. Finally, she stopped shaking and removed her hands. Charmaine passed her the tissue box, and Finn gratefully took a handful of tissues to wipe her eyes and blow her nose.

She smiled ruefully. "I can't believe she's gone. All this time, and I didn't know."

"I'm sorry to have to tell you," Charmaine said.

"I wondered at times. I hadn't heard from her in so long."

"I'm sure she missed you. She talked about you at the end, and that's how I knew where to look."

Finn sighed. "I wish I'd had a chance to say goodbye."

They spoke about Charmaine's mother and what her life had been. They discussed her grandparents and when they'd passed away, where they'd lived and how much they'd wished they could know their grandchildren.

"So, your last name is Edgeley?" Charmaine asked.

"Yes, it's my married name. My maiden name was Hilton."

"Does that mean Hilton is my real surname too?"

"Yes. Your mother never took your dad's name. You were both Hiltons, you and Sean. Until Helen moved away. She never told me what she ended up changing your names to. What was it?"

"Billings. I'm Charmaine Billings."

Finn laughed. "That's funny."

"Why is it funny?"

"Our childhood cat's name was Billings. Mr Billings, we called him. He was black and white, looked like he was wearing a suit, and he stalked around the place as if he were the butler."

Charmaine giggled. "That is funny. I'm named after a cat." She petted Watson's sleek back, then drew a long, slow breath.

"Will you tell me?"

"What's that?" Finn leaned against the back of the couch and tucked her feet beneath her.

"Tell me why. Mum would never tell me anything. I want to know why she left her family behind and changed our name. Why we never saw any of you again."

Finn's smile faded. She swallowed. "I don't know if you want to hear this. I've never told anyone."

"Please," Charmaine begged. "I've come all this way to find the truth. Mum is dead. There's no one left to protect."

"No one but you." Finn's jaw clenched.

"What could happen to me?" She was sincerely confused. What could've driven her mother away so long ago that might still be a threat to Charmaine's safety now?

Finn chewed on her lower lip. "Okay, fine. I suppose it doesn't matter now. So much time has passed. I'm the only one left who knows."

"Thank you," Charmaine said with relief. "I have to know the truth."

"Before I tell you, whatever happened to your brother?"

Charmaine sighed. "He's still hanging around. Unfortunately, he's not the man I hoped he'd be. He managed to fool Mum while she was alive, but he's not someone I trust. Not anymore."

"He didn't fool your mother as much as you thought he did. She sent me letters every now and then. I know she was worried about him. She worried about you, too. She thought you weren't strong enough to handle the hardships of life without her — she called you her sweet girl. But it seems to me you're tougher than she knew."

Charmaine choked back a sob. "I don't know about 'tough.' But I'm getting better with each day."

"That's all any of us can do. Let's see..." Finn played with her hair, flicking it behind her ears with her fingertips. "A long time ago, when your mother was a girl living here on Coral Island, she witnessed a crime. A friend of the family was babysitting her. She'd objected, saying she wasn't a baby and didn't need anyone to watch her, but my mother wouldn't listen. They'd gone to the mainland to meet with an accountant, and they didn't want to leave Helen at home alone. I went with them because I was a baby. Mum pushed me onto the ferry in my pram."

"What kind of crime?" Charmaine asked, perched on the edge of the couch, breathless.

"A murder."

"A murder? Really?" Charmaine's thoughts whirled. A murder? Surely it couldn't be the same one she and her friends had been investigating since she arrived on the island.

"That's right — Mary Brown. It's the only murder on the island in my lifetime, so it was a big deal at the time. They tell me the whole island was in uproar. Of course, I don't recall any of it."

Charmaine's stomach tightened into a giant knot. "I can't believe this."

"She was terrified. A little girl, witnessing something so violent — it impacted her. She didn't process her feelings, didn't know how to deal with what she'd seen. She was scared all the time. My parents weren't sure what to do with her. There was a baby there too, but the baby didn't see anything from what I recall. She was sleeping at the time."

"Do you mean Penny St James?"

"Yes, that's her. Do you know her?"

"We're friends," Charmaine replied. This seemed impossible. It couldn't be true — her mother had witnessed Penny's grandmother's murder?

"Helen was hiding in a storage cupboard at the time. Mary had been playing hide-and-seek with her, trying to get her to cheer up. They were on the back porch of the beach house. There were slats in the door, and she saw right through them. But the killer couldn't see her—didn't know she was there. Penny was a baby, asleep in her cot in the nursery. Helen stayed in the cupboard even when Penny started crying. She was too scared to move. That's what she told me years later. Said the memories came back to her in flashes."

"I can't believe it. All this time, she never mentioned it. I didn't know. And when I arrived on the island, I met Penny and her friends. They're curious about the murder, trying to find out what happened. I thought it had nothing to do with me, that I was an outsider looking in."

"Your mother's statement was given to the police. But it seems they didn't believe her, or they didn't understand. I'm not sure what the communication breakdown was. She was young and they didn't take her testimony seriously — they didn't think her words could be used as evidence. And that was the end of it."

"That must've been so frustrating for her."

"It was, but she put it behind her for years. Until she was an adult. When she was pregnant with your brother, she started thinking about it all over again. She was angry that the perpetrator had gotten away with it, that no one had listened to her or believed her. It started to eat her up. She talked about it too much, and one day she received a death threat in the mail."

"A death threat?" Charmaine's stomach flipped. "What did it say?"

"I don't know exactly. Something about keeping quiet, that they knew where she lived. It freaked her out."

"Of course it did," Charmaine said with a nod. "Surely she could take that to the police."

"She did, but they couldn't determine where the letter came from. This was the early eighties. There were no forensic investigators, no surveillance video footage. And no one had witnessed the person who put it in our mailbox. Your father was livid, but there wasn't much anyone could do."

"Poor Mum," Charmaine said with a sigh as she scratched behind Watson's ears. "Is that when she left?"

"No, that wasn't until years later after her divorce. We all thought she'd given up on it. I realise now, it was what she wanted us to believe. She must've kept working on the mystery in secret because one day after you were born and your father had left, she came home from a long walk very excited. She'd found something, she said. Something that would prove her right. Something important."

Charmaine leaned forwards. "What was it?"

Finn shook her head. "She never told me. She left soon after that, moved away. She came home a couple of times and brought you kids with her, but then she got spooked and changed her name, moved again and never came back. As I said, she sent me the occasional message, but otherwise, we didn't hear from her. It was a source of great pain for my parents up until they died. They wanted nothing more than for all of you to come home and be part of the family again. They thought they'd failed in some way. They didn't understand why she did it."

"But you understood?"

Finn exhaled a long, deep breath. "I can look back now and see why — she wanted to keep you and your brother safe. After the history she had with the police, them not believing her or protecting her, she didn't feel as though she could count on them. She always said the Coral Island Police were as useful as a sea sponge."

Charmaine laughed. "That's a bit harsh."

Finn shrugged. "It was her experience."

"So, you have no idea what she discovered?"

"None, but whatever it was, it meant something to the murderer because we kept getting hang-ups on the phone for years after she left, and every now and then I'd see footprints in the backyard first thing in the morning. Someone broke in once and ransacked the whole house. Mum and Dad thought it was a robbery, but nothing was taken. I always believed it was the murderer looking for whatever it was that Helen found."

Eighteen

EVIE SAT in the *Coral Café*, waiting for Beatrice. She missed Penny and Taya. Penny had been gone for two weeks, travelling the world with Rowan. She'd heard from her a few times and so far, the messages had been positive, but Evie wanted desperately to see her friend and ask if she was genuinely okay. Taya was travelling for work, although she expected to be back on the island the following week. So, it was only going to be Bea and Evie catching up for coffee, since Charmaine was busy working at *Betsy's Florals*. And the only place left where they could find a coffee was the *Coral Café*.

The drab establishment was owned by Rowan's mother, June Clements, and didn't have an espresso machine, much to Evie's dismay. She cupped a coffee with both hands and stared into its dark depths. It wasn't the good stuff, but it would have to do. June set a lamington on the table before her with a small fork balanced on the edge of the plate. The square cake looked festive, with coconut sprinkled over the chocolate icing. "Is that all?"

"Yes, thanks, June. Beatrice should be here soon."

"I was sorry to see what happened to your bookshop and her café. I liked both businesses." June didn't speak often, and certainly not to say something nice.

Evie looked at her in surprise. "Thanks, June. I appreciate it."

She nodded and then returned to her place behind the counter to wipe down surfaces.

David was walking past the café when he waved at her through the large glass window. He came in through the front door and strode over to her table.

"Hi. I wasn't expecting to run into you today."

She patted the seat next to hers. "Do you have time to sit? I'm meeting Bea, but I'm early if you'd like to grab a coffee and share my lamington."

"I'd love that." He ordered a coffee and an extra fork, then pulled his chair closer to her. "What's that?"

"My insurance claim. I'm writing down valuable books, the new bookshelves—anything that might help me get a higher settlement. I'm only now realising just how disorganised I am. It's irritating."

"Do you need some help?"

"Yes, please," she replied.

As she flicked through photographs on her phone and tapped her way through files on her iPad, she talked about the items to include on the list, and the stone of sadness in her gut grew.

"This is painful," she said.

He sipped his coffee. "I can't imagine. This was your dream, and it's gone. You've clearly put so much effort into curating an amazing collection of books."

"And some artwork, too," she added.

"And art," he agreed. "I hate that it's been destroyed like this."

"It all happened so fast." Her throat tightened. "I'd forgotten about some of these books. They were special—some limited editions, some autographed. I can never get them back."

He rested a hand over hers. "I'm so sorry. I wish there was something I could do."

"Me too," Evie replied. "But there's nothing anyone can do now. It helps that you're here though." She patted his hand.

"I talked to my students about your fire and used it as an example of how unexpected things can happen in life."

"I hope you didn't scare them."

"No, I tried to keep it light. But they were interested, since they've all seen the building since the fire. They wanted to talk about it. It helps for them to be able to process things that happen. This fire has impacted everyone in the community."

Evie took a bite of lamington. The chocolate and coconut blended together and complemented her coffee nicely. Just then, Bea arrived with Aidan. They stepped through the door and greeted Evie and David, then ordered coffee and cakes. Evie ordered another drink, this time a tea.

"I miss your café," Evie whispered across the table.

Bea sighed. "I know. Me too."

They chatted about their families and what was going on in their lives for a few minutes before Bea raised the topic they'd met to discuss.

"We need to talk about our businesses," she said.

Evie nodded and pushed the empty lamington plate to the side. "I suppose the first question we should both answer is, do we want to rebuild?"

Bea exchanged a glance with Aidan. "I've thought about this a lot, and I've decided I don't want to start over again. I might buy an existing café in the future and keep it as an investment rather than running it on my own. I've learned so much about the business and how to be successful, I'd hate to lose all of that knowledge and experience. But for now, I have no desire to rebuild my business. I loved that place, I put everything into it, and it's gone."

Evie gaped. She hadn't expected that of Beatrice. She knew how much her friend enjoyed running the café and had thought she'd never walk away it. Not after how hard she'd worked to build up her customer base and her roster of experienced staff.

"I'm sorry to hear that." Evie bit down on her lower lip. She wanted to cry. Her heart broke for Bea and what they'd each lost.

Bea reached for Aidan's hand and laced her fingers through his. "It's okay. I'm going to be fine. Aidan has decided to take an extended leave from his job. Of course, David already knows that since he's Aidan's new boss."

David smiled. "What will you do with the time off?"

"We're going to travel. We've always wanted to, and now we have the opportunity," Aidan replied.

Bea added. "I couldn't have left the café unattended for long and even though I'm sad over losing it, I'm choosing instead to see it as our chance to do all the things we've dreamed of doing. Right, honey?"

Aidan kissed the tip of her nose. "That's right. We're going to see the world and have some adventures, and when we come back, maybe we'll pick up where we left off, or maybe we'll do something completely new and different. But we've got plenty of time to think about it."

Evie shook her head. "I think I've come to the same conclusion. I don't want to start over again. It's too hard, all of it. I'm devastated, but also a little bit excited about the idea of doing something different. I'm sad for my staff, especially Janice. But she told me not to worry, she'd find something else.

And Bradford offered me a job, so I think I'm going to take it."

"What? Really?" Bea cocked her head to one side. "Brad offered you a job? What kind of job?"

"He's opening an office here on the island. He's going to find out if our landlord will let him build it on the site."

"That's a great idea," Aidan said.

"He's asked me to run it. I think it might be fun. Besides, it's so much easier than managing my own business. I'll get a paycheck and holidays. Imagine that!"

Bea laughed. "It sounds good. That's a big relief. I was worried about you. I thought I was letting you down by walking away, but now I'll be able to finally let it go."

"You're not letting me down," Evie assured her. "It's probably time for me to do something new. I've done the same thing for so long that I don't know where to begin making changes in my life, but I'm going to try."

Everything was changing. Some of the items she'd lost in the fire were irreplaceable. Some were sentimental, others valuable. But the biggest thing she'd lost was her confidence — the feeling that the future was solid and her life path was well established. That feeling was gone, and instead, she'd been shaken to her core. The fights with her sister, their reconciliation, the loss of the bookshop and darkroom—all of it had left the ground beneath her feet unstable. She looked at David, who rested a hand on her back. She could get used to having him around — another new thing to adjust to, but one she hoped to enjoy for a long time.

"I almost forgot," David said. "I have something for you which is pertinent given the conversation we've just had."

He reached to the floor and pulled a shoulder bag into his lap, opened it and tugged out a large fabric bag. He opened the bag and slid a book out onto the table.

Evie stared at it, reading, then her eyes widened. She

picked it up gingerly and flipped through a few of the pages. "Is this a first addition signed copy of 'Playing Beatie Beau'?"

He grinned. "Yep."

"How did you get this?" She turned it over, admiring the cover and the perfectly clean pages. "It still looks brand new."

"I bought it a long time ago for a friend, but I never gave it to her. I was going through some boxes and thought you might like to have it."

She sighed. "No, I can't accept it. It's too much. You should keep it."

He waved her off. "It's not very much. You've lost everything, and I'd only store it in a box if I keep it."

"It's one of my favourite books," she said.

Bea laughed. "I remember reading that in year seven. I loved it because it's almost my name in the title."

"Thank you," Evie said, emotion welling in her throat. "This means a lot to me."

"I hope you enjoy it, and maybe it can remind you of the bookshop. One day, that memory will be a happy one."

Evie patted the back cover with her hand and then slid the book back into its protective bag. "One day."

How had David known this gift would be exactly what she needed? In all the years of working at the bookshop, the stress, the schedules, and the customers, somewhere along the line she'd lost her love of books. She'd still enjoyed them, of course, and was excited to open new boxes of them to line her shelves, but the childlike passion for a first-edition copy of one of her favourites had been replaced with spreadsheets, balancing the books, making a profit and finding the next big novel to fly off the shelves.

She slipped her hand into his and squeezed, unable to find the words to express how she felt. He seemed to understand and dipped his head towards her.

Charmaine stepped into the café, glancing around until her gaze landed on Evie and the others at the table.

"Hi, Chaz. Want to sit with us?" Bea asked.

Evie patted the empty chair beside her. "Grab a seat."

"Hi," Chaz replied, eyeing the chair. "Um... okay. I guess I can stay a minute."

She sat hesitantly, her back straight.

"How're things?" Aidan asked.

Charmaine sighed. "I wanted to let you all know that I think Sean has left the island. I asked him to, and I haven't seen him since. I stopped in at the motel where he was staying, and they said he checked out last week. So, it seems like he's gone."

"Okay," Evie replied.

"I wanted to tell you so you wouldn't worry. The police needed to speak to him about the fire, but I believe he left town before they had a chance. I told him to go in for an interview, and I'm still hoping he will do that. He says he's innocent, but we won't know for sure until the police finish their investigation."

Charmaine's tone was formal. Her gaze darted from face to face and then to the table and back again. Her hands were linked together in her lap.

"I know we already said this, but it's not your fault, you know..." Evie said.

Charmaine glanced at her. "Thanks."

"It's not," Bea agreed.

"I shouldn't have come to book club," Charmaine said, raising her hands in surrender. "It's my fault he was there."

"He's responsible for his own actions, not you."

"I could've dealt with it sooner. I've given him what he wanted, and he's gone. I wish I'd done it the first time he asked."

"What did he want?" David asked.

"Money," Charmaine said simply. "I don't want to talk about it, but he's gone now, and I thought you should know."

"Thanks for telling us," Evie said.

Charmaine nodded then walked away. She turned back at the last moment to study them all. "I'm sorry. You've all been so kind to me, welcomed me into your hearts and lives, and this is how you've been repaid."

Then she was gone. The door swung shut behind her. Evie stared at the place where she'd been moments earlier. She'd had no idea Charmaine was still blaming herself for the fire. It was most likely an accident, but if it'd been caused by her brother, that wasn't something she should blame herself over. She ran after Charmaine, through the door and along the street.

"Chaz! Wait!" She reached her and embraced her, then stepped back to look her in the eye. "Please don't let this thing come between our friendship."

Bea caught up to them, puffing lightly.

"I don't know what to do," Charmaine said, pressing her hands to her hips.

"Your brother is abusive and manipulative and he's responsible for his own choices." Evie shook her head. "My sister did some cruel things to me and the other people in her life, and for a long time, I blamed myself for what happened. Why didn't I see it sooner? How could I let her take the man I loved and ruin the life I'd planned for myself? Why wasn't I stronger, more forceful? I should've communicated better, or seen it coming. But in the end, I realised that she'd done those things, not me. I wasn't to blame. And you're not responsible for your brother either."

Charmaine's eyes were full of sadness. "I'm sorry about your sister. I didn't realise."

"It was a long time ago, and we've made amends."

Bea looped her arm through Evie's, then Charmaine's.

"We're all sisters now, not by blood but by choice. We're on your side."

Charmaine's eyes filled with tears.

"Come back and have coffee with us. We've got a lot to talk about," Evie said.

Charmaine gave a quick nod. "Okay."

Nineteen

CHARMAINE DECIDED NOT to leave Coral Island. She'd created a life for herself there and she wasn't going to let her brother scare her away from it. Even if she went somewhere else, he'd track her down and find her. She'd have to change her name and disappear if she was to be rid of him entirely. And besides, she'd set up a system she hoped would keep him away. If he came to see her without her permission, she'd cut off the funds that he desperately needed. It probably wouldn't work forever, but she hoped it would for now. At least until the police caught up with him.

She lifted the box from the back of Bradford's truck and carried it into the beach cottage. Then she stood with both hands on her hips, out of breath, to survey the work they'd done.

It was a blessing that Bea had left most of the furniture and appliances in the cottage, since Charmaine didn't have any of her own. She only had a few boxes of things and her push bike, so moving had been a breeze.

"That's everything," Bradford said, setting her bike against the outside wall of the house and stepping through the kitchen door behind her.

"Thanks for your help," Charmaine replied. "I'm going to love it here. I can just tell."

"I think you will too." He linked his arms around her waist, and she spun in his embrace to stand on tiptoe and kiss his lips.

He held her tight against him, his lips moving in motion with hers.

"You two should get a room," Finn said, wiping her boots on the mat. "Oh, wait. You have a whole cottage. Never mind."

Charmaine took a step back and out of Bradford's arms, her face flushed with heat. "Hi, Auntie Finn. I wasn't expecting you."

"Clearly." Finn winked. "I got you a housewarming gift."

She handed Charmaine a blender. "It's not much, but I thought you might like to make a smoothie for breakfast occasionally."

"Thanks. You didn't have to do that."

Finn waved a hand. "It's what aunties do, and I have a lot of catching up to cover. The kids want you to come over for dinner tonight — unless you'd rather stay here. We can make it another night." She eyed Bradford with a grin.

"That would be perfect. I haven't been to the shops yet, and I don't have anything to eat here." Charmaine could tell she was going to enjoy having a family again.

Bradford leaned close to kiss her goodbye. "I've got to get moving. I have a client meeting. But I'll call later. Okay?"

She nodded and waved goodbye through the back screen door. When he was gone, she sighed and turned to find Finn watching her with interest.

"He's a good one," Finn said.

Charmaine set the blender in a cupboard. "Seems like it."

"I'm happy for you both. Now come into the living room, I've got something I have to show you."

* * *

When Charmaine was seated on the couch, Finn sat beside her. She pulled a small box out of her shoulder bag and set it on the coffee table. The box was old and peeling. When she opened the lid, Charmaine peered inside, but couldn't see anything particularly interesting.

"What is it?"

"After Helen left home, I was curious and looked in her room. This was the only thing I found."

Finn pulled an old, dull-looking ring out of the box. The ring was large enough to fit a woman's finger, but there was nothing in the setting. "I honestly don't know why I kept this thing all these years. It's not worth anything. There must've been a stone in the setting a long time ago. I often wondered why Helen had it hidden in her closet."

She handed the ring to Charmaine, who turned it over and examined it closely. It was made of gold, although it was so tarnished, it was hard to tell. The setting was large, and she suddenly remembered the diamond they'd discovered in the cave the day they'd followed Betsy down the cliffs.

"Wait here." She went to her room and found the box with her personal care items against one wall. She cut it open with a box cutter she'd stuffed into her back jeans pocket earlier. She'd stowed her mother's jewels at the bank, but the diamond they found in the cave, she'd left with her other costume jewellery. It was dull and lifeless and looked like a piece of cubic zirconia. Anyone searching through the box would never guess it was a diamond. In fact, Charmaine wasn't certain it was.

She carried it out to the living room and set it on top of the ring. Finn gasped.

Charmaine's heart skipped a beat. The diamond fit the setting perfectly.

"Where on earth did you find that?" Finn asked.

"It's a long story. Did you ever ask Mum about the ring?"

"She called here once from a public phone years after you left. I mentioned the ring and she said she left it behind because it didn't have the diamond, but that she had other jewellery and it was worth a lot of money."

"Did she tell you anything else about it?"

"Just that she'd taken it from the murderer's lair, or something equally dramatic. It sounded like a fantasy story and honestly, there were times when I wondered if she'd made up the entire thing. But I had the ring and so I'd sit and stare at it, wondering who it belonged to and what it all meant."

Charmaine set the ring and diamond on the coffee table and tucked her legs up beneath her on the couch. "It's all so confusing."

"Apparently, she did some research right before she left Coral Island and discovered that the killer had come to the island after stealing the diamond jewellery from a bank overseas. At least, she thought that's what had happened. She didn't have any proof, of course, so when she suggested to the police that the killer was in fact also a robber, she said they laughed her out of the station. They needed evidence, they said. She planned on going back to the station the next day with the jewellery, but that night someone broke into the house and threatened her. She didn't tell them where the jewellery was, and my parents came home early and scared the person off. Helen left the island the next day. She said she couldn't risk your safety, or Sean's."

Charmaine's head spun with the new information. How she wished her mother had done things differently. It seemed there were so many ways she could've handled the situation better, and maybe they'd all have had a family they could rely on.

"Why didn't she take the jewellery to the police on the mainland?"

"I don't know. We can look back now and have a different perspective, but she was alone, scared and inexperienced. She only knew she had to keep the two of you safe."

"Did she ever tell you the name of the killer?"

Finn shook her head. "She wouldn't say. She didn't want to put me or our parents in danger."

Charmaine sighed. "I have a feeling someone I care about knows the truth."

Twenty

IT SEEMED impossible for Charmaine to find out where the diamond jewellery had come from. The time frame was too long ago. There were several mentions of jewellery heists in the old newspapers at the library, but none that matched the items she'd found. She flicked though the images on the computer screen. Then with a frustrated grunt, she collected her purse and headed for the door.

She was thinking through everything she'd seen, when she heard shouting in the florist shop ahead. She stopped before she reached the doorway and peered around the corner and through the window.

Frank was there, yelling at Betsy again. A pit formed in Charmaine's stomach. She hated conflict more than anything, and lately Frank and Betsy had been getting along better. She'd hoped they'd moved past the constant arguing and bickering, the yelling matches and the storming out. But he was back, and his voice echoed low in the small shop. Thankfully there were no customers.

Charmaine glanced around. There were a few people on the street, but no one looking at the florist's. Should she go inside? It might only make things worse. If Frank acted the way he usually did, he'd shout at Betsy, then storm through the front door and leave. Betsy would be fine. She was a tough old lady, something Charmaine had grown to admire about her.

She moved past the doorway and sat with her ear up against the window. They wouldn't see her from inside, since there were potted plants in the way, but she could hear when Frank was coming and keep from being bowled over by the door.

There was a bang, like someone slapped a palm down hard on a table.

"Frank, stop!" Betsy's voice was low, measured.

"I can't stop, Mum, because I've spent my whole life wondering if you care about me. And now I know the truth. It says here that a boy called Frank was kidnapped by a Betsy Alton. The woman in the photo looks remarkably similar to the photos you had pinned up all around your shop. Is this you, Mum?"

Betsy mumbled something incoherent, her tone reassuring.

"Stop it! You can't keep telling me these lies, Mum. I'm not a little boy anymore. I was right all along, wasn't I? All those years when I didn't believe you cared and I wondered if something was wrong because your stories didn't add up, I was right! This is why we've never been able to have a solid relationship, why I don't trust you. I never knew the truth about my past or about our lives. I could tell something was wrong, but I didn't know exactly what it was. I only knew you weren't truthful. Then, when you lied for Buck, it all became so real. You were a liar — you lied then, and you're lying now. You took me, stole me. I'm the Frank from this article, aren't I?"

Betsy was silent. The world around Charmaine began to

spin. All this time, she'd been certain that Bea, Evie and Penny were wrong about Betsy. It couldn't be true—the stories had to be about someone else. She'd gone along with them because it was exciting and interesting, but it wasn't real life. Not the life she knew, or the woman she'd grown to love as a grandmother.

Betsy grunted. "Frank, honey, you don't understand. It's a long story, and now isn't the time. Sam's in the other room, and I don't want her to hear. But I do owe you the truth. If you'll give me a chance, I'll explain everything. Just not now. I need to think, to find the words, and I can't do that with Sam here."

"All my life, you said we were from Indiana, but this article claims the boy who was taken is from California. So, which is it, Mum? Are we from California? Are you Betsy Alton or Betsy Norton? What is my real name, Mother? And why did you take me away from my home to a small tropical island on the other side of the world?"

"Where did you find these?" Betsy asked.

Frank laughed. "That's what you're worried about? I found them in here. I came by the other night for Sam, but you'd already left with her. Chaz was here, working late. She left the articles on this table to look for Sam's homework out back."

Betsy hesitated. Charmaine's stomach tightened into a knot. The tone of Betsy's voice scared her when she spoke.

"She must be on to me. Did she say anything? Think, Frank! I have to know what Chaz knows."

"On to what, Mum? You've got to tell me what's going on. I'm all grown up. Why can't you trust me with your secrets?"

"I trust you, but I don't want to burden you. The truth is a millstone around your neck. The police will use it against you, against our family."

"I'm not going to betray you, Mum. Don't you know me at all?"

A chair scraped across the floor. Finally, Betsy spoke. "I'll tell you everything, but you have to promise to keep it quiet."

He mumbled a faint response.

"I did it all for you. Everything I've done was to keep you safe. Your father was a cruel man, and he wouldn't have left us alone. Not ever. I had to bring you here."

"Did he look for us?"

"Every day until he died," Betsy replied.

Frank's voice was soft now. "I could've had a father."

"Not one you'd have wanted."

"You chase away everyone who loves me. First my father, then my wife. Why? Do you want me to be alone?"

There was silence for several long moments. Charmaine held her breath. Her heart ached for Frank and the pain he'd lived with for so long.

"I didn't have a choice, Frank. We had to leave. Your dad wasn't good to us. Your wife didn't love you. I did what I had to do."

Frank's volume rose. "You didn't have to chase my wife away. She loved me and Sam. She was good for us. She had problems, but I was ready to deal with them. That's what marriage is about — you love each other through the hard times. I could've gotten help for her, for us. We should've gone to counselling—that's what I was going to suggest. But she left because you couldn't stand for me to have someone in my life who made me happy. Someone other than you."

"I can't believe you'd say that," Betsy growled. "You're an ungrateful child. You always have been."

"Grateful? Why should I be grateful? What have you ever done to give me a life I should be grateful for?"

"I kept you safe, I gave up everything to move to this island for you. My whole life has been about protecting you and providing for you. I built a business, I fed you, I clothed you. Have you ever been hungry or frightened? No!"

Frank slammed a fist down on the table. The sound vibrated against Charmaine's ear, and she jumped away from the window for a moment. With a hand to her mouth, she returned to her position, listening.

"I've lived in fear most of my life because the man you call my uncle is a murderer. We've eaten with him, spent time at his house, but you act as though he's done nothing wrong. He could kill us in our sleep. What about Sam? What if he comes after her the way he did that poor woman?"

"Be quiet, Frank. You don't know what you're talking about, and someone might hear you."

Frank lowered his voice. "What about Dad? Did he know the truth?"

Betsy mumbled something Charmaine couldn't hear. Then her voice grew higher. "Your father was a harsh man. I'm sorry to have to say it. I've tried to shield you from that all this time, but it's the truth."

"What? What did he do?"

"He was a criminal and a thug. Listen—this is all in the past, Frank. Let it go. It's behind us. Your uncle is innocent, your father was conniving, just like your wife, and I'm the only one who truly loves you. These are the facts. You need to hold on to the facts and not let anyone lie to you about what really happened. I'm your mother. You must always believe family first."

"I don't know what to believe, Mum." Frank's voice wobbled. "I can't separate the truth from the lies. My whole life has been a mess of confusion, fabrications, secrets and stories. Buck did it. I know he did. The only question I have is, why? Why would he kill that woman?"

Betsy's voice sounded tired through the pane of glass. "He didn't."

"What?"

"He didn't kill her. I've said it a hundred times, but you never listen. He didn't hurt Mary Brown. He's innocent."

"Then why did the police arrest him? Why do they believe he's the murderer?"

There was a pause. And when Betsy's voice cut through the silence, it sent a chill up Charmaine's spine.

"Because I wanted them to believe it."

* * *

Continue the series...

Ready to read book 6 in the *Coral Island* series so you can keep following Beatrice, Aidan and the rest of the Coral Island crew? Buy the next book in this series!

Want to find out about all of my new releases? You can get on my VIP reader list by subscribing via my website, and you'll also get a free book.

Also by Lilly Mirren

WOMEN'S FICTION

CORAL ISLAND SERIES

The Island

After twenty five years of marriage and decades caring for her two children, on the evening of their vow renewal, her husband shocks her with the news that he's leaving her.

The Beach Cottage

Beatrice is speechless. It's something she never expected — a secret daughter. She and Aidan have only just renewed their romance, after decades apart, and he never mentioned a child. Did he know she existed?

The Blue Shoal Inn

Taya's inn is in trouble. Her father has built a fancy new resort in Blue Shoal and hired a handsome stranger to manage it. When the stranger offers to buy her inn and merge it with the resort, she wants to hate him but when he rescues a stray dog her feelings for him change.

Island Weddings

Charmaine moves to Coral Island and lands a job working at a local florist shop. It seems as though the entire island has caught wedding fever, with weddings planned every weekend. It's a good opportunity for her to get to know the locals, but what she doesn't expect is to be thrown into the middle of a family drama.

The Island Bookshop

Evie's book club friends are the people in the world she relies on most. But when one of the newer members finds herself confronted with her past, the rest of the club will do what they can to help, endangering the existence of the bookshop without realising it.

An Island Reunion

It's been thirty five years since the friends graduated from Coral Island State Primary School and the class is returning to the island to celebrate. A reunion can mean only one thing — Coral Island's secrets and lies will finally unravel and the truth will be revealed.

THE WARATAH INN SERIES

The Waratah Inn

Wrested back to Cabarita Beach by her grandmother's sudden death, Kate Summer discovers a mystery buried in the past that changes everything.

One Summer in Italy

Reeda leaves the Waratah Inn and returns to Sydney, her

husband, and her thriving interior design business, only to find her marriage in tatters. She's lost sight of what she wants in life and can't recognise the person she's become.

The Summer Sisters

Set against the golden sands and crystal clear waters of Cabarita Beach three sisters inherit an inn and discover a mystery about their grandmother's past that changes everything they thought they knew about their family...

Christmas at The Waratah Inn

Liz Cranwell is divorced and alone at Christmas. When her friends convince her to holiday at The Waratah Inn, she's dreading her first Christmas on her own. Instead she discovers that strangers can be the balm to heal the wounds of a lonely heart in this heartwarming Christmas story.

EMERALD COVE SERIES

Cottage on Oceanview Lane

When a renowned book editor returns to her roots, she rediscovers her strength & her passion in this heartwarming novel.

Seaside Manor Bed & Breakfast

The Seaside Manor Bed and Breakfast has been an institution in Emerald Cove for as long as anyone can remember. But things are changing and Diana is nervous about what the future might hold for her and her husband, not to mention the historic business.

Bungalow on Pelican Way

Moving to the Cove gave Rebecca De Vries a place to hide from her abusive ex. Now that he's in jail, she can get back to living her life as a police officer in her adopted hometown working alongside her intractable but very attractive boss, Franklin.

Chalet on Cliffside Drive

At forty-four years of age, Ben Silver thought he'd never find love. When he moves to Emerald Cove, he does it to support his birth mother, Diana, after her husband's sudden death. But then he meets Vicky.

An Emerald Cove Christmas

The Flannigan family has been through a lot together. They've grown and changed over the years and now have a blended and extended family that doesn't always see eye to eye. But this Christmas they'll learn that love can overcome all of the pain and differences of the past in this inspiring Christmas tale.

HOME SWEET HOME SERIES

Home Sweet Home

Trina is starting over after a painful separation from her husband of almost twenty years. Grief and loss force her to return to her hometown where she has to deal with all of the things she left behind to rebuild her life, piece by piece; a hometown she hasn't visited since high school graduation.

No Place Like Home

Lisa never thought she'd leave her high-profile finance job in the city to work in a small-town bakery. She also never expected to still be single in her forties.

HISTORICAL FICTION

Beyond the Crushing Waves

An emotional standalone historical saga. Two children plucked from poverty & forcibly deported from the UK to Australia. Inspired by true events. An unforgettable tale of loss, love, redemption & new beginnings.

Under a Sunburnt Sky

Inspired by a true story. Jan Kostanski is a normal Catholic boy in Warsaw when the nazis invade. He's separated from his neighbours, a Jewish family who he considers kin, by the ghetto wall. Jan and his mother decide that they will do whatever it takes to save their Jewish friends from certain death. The unforgettable tale of an everyday family's fight against evil, and the unbreakable bonds of their love.

MYSTERIES

White Picket Lies

Fighting the demons of her past Toni finds herself in the midst of a second marriage breakdown at forty seven years of age. She struggles to keep depression at bay while doing her best to raise a wayward teenaged son and uncover the identity of the killer.

In this small town investigation, it's only a matter of time until friends and neighbours turn on each other.

Cast of Characters

As the *Coral Island* series grows, the cast of characters does too. I hope this handy reference will help you keep them sorted!

* * *

Aidan Whitlock - former professional footballer, current primary school PE teacher.

Andrew Reddy - The new manager at *Paradise Resort*.

Annie Draper - Bea's friend from Sydney.

Beatrice Rushton - previously married and living in Sydney, now a resident of Coral Island.

Betsy Norton - Elderly, American, owns the florist shop.

Bradford Rushton - Bea's younger brother, owns a charter fishing company out of Airlie Beach.

Brett O'Hanley - Beatrice & Aidan's contractor.

Buck Clements - Rowan's step father and June's ex-husband.

Camden Futcher - Taya's adult daughter, training to become a chef in Cairns.

Cameron Eldridge - Taya's father and owner of *Paradise Resorts*.

Charmaine Billings - new resident of Coral Island, works at Betsy's Florals.

Damien Lachey - Dani's boyfriend, the professor and architect.

Danita Pike - Bea's adult daughter, lives in Sydney

David Ackerman - Principal at the Coral Island primary school

Elias Rushton - Bea's father, lives on Coral Island.

Emily Johson - Evie Mair's twin sister

Eveleigh (Evie) Mair - Owner of *Eveleigh's Books*, the book shop attached the *Bea's Coffee*.

Finn Edgeley - Watson, the cat's, official owner.

Frank Norton - Betsy's adult son and Samantha's father.

Fudge - Beatrice's pug.

Gareth Johnson - Emily's husband (Evie's brother in law)

Grace Allen - Aidan's teenaged daughter.

Harry Pike - Bea's adult son, lives in Sydney.

Henry St James - Penny's stepfather, married to Ruby St James.

Jacqui St James - Rob St James' estranged wife.

Julian St James - Rob's young son.

June Clements - proprietor of the *Coral Cafe* & Rowan's mother.

Kelly Allen - Grace's mother & Aidan's ex-girlfriend.

Luella Rushton - Bea's mother, deceased.

Mary Brown - Penny's grandmother, murder victim.

Ms Gossamer - librarian in Kellyville.

Penny St James - Owner of the *Coral Island Wildlife Rescue Centre*.

Preston Pike - Bea's ex-husband, lives between Sydney & Melbourne.

Robert St James - Penny's brother, travels around to work in construction.

Rowan Clements - June Clements' son, journalist.

Ruby St James - Penny's mother.

Samantha Norton - Betsy's granddaughter & Frank's daughter.

Samuel Jay Gilmore - the name on Buck's California driver's license.

Sean Billings - Charmaine's brother.

Taya Eldridge - Owns the Blue Shoal Inn, is Cameron & Tina Eldridge's daughter.

Tina Eldridge - Taya's mother, married to Cameron.

Todd Futcher - Taya's former husband, deceased.

Watson - Charmaine's visiting cat.

About the Author

Lilly Mirren is an Amazon top 20, Audible top 15 and USA Today Bestselling author who has sold over one million copies of her books worldwide. She lives in Brisbane, Australia with her husband and three children.

She always dreamed of being a writer and is now living that dream. Her books combine heartwarming storylines with realistic characters readers can't get enough of.

Her debut series, The Waratah Inn, set in the delightful Cabarita Beach, hit the *USA Today* Bestseller list and since then, has touched the hearts of hundreds of thousands of readers across the globe.

32634132R00121